SYNOPSIS

Two years after losing his husband, the last thing widower Rob Asher wants to do is go on a cruise-for-two by himself. But after some practical advice from his best friend, Rob realizes that his husband wouldn't have wanted him to hide away from the world with only his grief for company. So despite some lingering doubts, Rob packs his bags for his cruise adventure and flies to Barcelona to board the *Ocean Wanderer*.

Actor Ben Rockingham has just finished a whirlwind promotional tour around Europe and is looking forward to a week long cruise so he can relax and unwind. He's felt alone for far too long and doesn't foresee that changing anytime soon. But a chance encounter in a hotel bar has Ben feeling things he hasn't contemplated for a very long time.

He and Rob hit it off right away and Ben is both intrigued by and attracted to this conflicted man. Is it possible that Rob is the one who's been missing from Ben's life all these years, and can Ben help Rob move past his grief so they have a chance at a future together? They have one week aboard the *Ocean Wanderer* to find out and the stakes are high on the high seas.

Love ON THE HORIZON

NEW ADVENTURES IN LOVE · BOOK 1

RJ Peterson

No Generative AI Training Use.

For avoidance of doubt, Author reserves the rights, and does not grant permission to any individual/company/publisher/platform any rights to reproduce and/or otherwise use the Work in any manner for purposes of training artificial intelligence technologies to generate text, including without limitation, technologies that are capable of generating works in the same style or genre as the Work, unless said individual/company/publisher/platform obtains Author's specific and express permission to do so. Nor does any individual/company/publisher/platform have the right to sublicense others to reproduce and/or otherwise use the Work in any manner for purposes of training artificial intelligence technologies to generate text without Author's specific and express permission.

In addition, no artificial intelligence (A.I.), predictive language software, or generative design software was used in any part of the creation of this book or its cover, nor will it ever be for any of my works.

To David

Thank you for traveling with me on this journey called life.

"In life, it's not where you go. It's who you travel with."

– Charles Schulz

CONTENTS

ACKNOWLEDGMENTS

There are so many people who helped make this book possible; I can't thank you all enough.

Karen D. Bonnick, my friend, mentor, and colleague - I could *not* have done this without you. Thank you for your guidance and encouragement throughout the process.

Dianne Thies, endless thanks for putting up with this newbie author and taking me under your editorial wing. You helped me in so many ways and I'm forever grateful.

Sharon Hamner, my BFF - you are my Sam! We've had lots of fun times over the years and I'm sure there'll be more to come. I hope you had fun being a part of Rob & Ben's story.

Melissa Brus, your friendship and support are beyond measure. I owe you hugs...and tequila!

T.S. McKinney, you're crazy and I love you. Thank you for believing in me. And yes, I owe you alcohol, too!

Brandon Witt-Schoen, thanks for letting me borrow The Cozy Corgi Mysteries and Mildred Abbott so that Ben had something to read. Your friendship and constant support means so very much to me.

My beta-team: Sammi Cee, Jenn L. Gibson, K-Lee Klein, Reese Knightley, Annabella Michaels, Tricia Morris, & Deanna Wadsworth – this book is immeasurably better because of your input. Thank you from the bottom of my heart.

Special thanks to Ana, Bernadette, Betty, Cheryl, Darlene, Lucy, Shaz & Shona for suggesting sea-related names for public spaces aboard *Ocean Wanderer*. I haven't used them all yet, but there will be more books and more ships.

All the authors who have inspired and entertained me over the years: Gregory Ashe, Tal Bauer, Hank Edwards, Rhys Ford, Jordan L. Hawk, Davidson King, Alexa Land, Ann Lister, Angel Martinez, C.S. Poe, and so many more – huge thanks for the laughter, tears, & angst. And most important, thank you for your friendship and support.

PROLOGUE

"Please return your seat backs and tray tables to their full upright and locked positions and ensure that your seat belts are securely fastened," the flight attendant said over the plane's PA system. "We'll be landing at Barcelona-El Prat Airport in just a few minutes."

Rob rubbed at the knot behind his right shoulder and moaned quietly. He was exhausted. While he had managed to sleep a bit during the overnight flight from Boston to London, the flight from London to Barcelona was too short for more. And besides, he never slept well on a plane, even when he could stretch out in business class. Fortunately, an in-flight movie and his Kindle had kept him occupied for the majority of the longer flight. Hopefully his room would be ready when he got to the hotel and he could crash for a few hours. He sighed inwardly. Was he doing the right thing flying here and getting on a cruise ship? Alan had been gone for two years. This was the trip they'd planned together and now his husband wasn't here to enjoy it with him. Maybe he should have just stayed home.

But no, damn it! He promised Samantha that he'd make this trip even if it was without Alan. He'd agreed not to hide in his room either in Barcelona or on the cruise. Rob was relieved that she'd be joining him for most of this trip because that's what BFFs were for, right? He could manage to spend a few days in Barcelona and then a week on the cruise by himself. After that, Sam would be with him and they'd cruise together for fourteen nights, seeing a bit of Europe, then crossing the Atlantic before finally arriving in Fort Lauderdale.

Gathering his backpack and carry-on, Rob stood with a groan, feeling every one of his fifty-eight years. Okay, he wasn't old, but some days he certainly felt that way. He got off the plane and made his way to baggage claim without any difficulty, though it felt strange to be doing so alone.

Stop it, he scolded himself, *you can do this.*

It took a few minutes for his checked bag to show up on the baggage carousel and once he retrieved it, Rob headed to customs. Fortunately, the line wasn't long and he got through it all very quickly. As he exited the doorway, he saw a group of drivers holding placards, or in some cases tablets, with last names on them and after a quick scan, he spotted a handsome young guy with an iPad that said Asher in bold letters.

Rob approached him with a smile and said, "I'm Robert Asher."

"*Buenos dias, señor Asher,*" the man said. "I am Eduardo."

Eduardo took his bags, leaving him with just his backpack and said, "Please follow me. My car is not far."

Although Rob knew a smattering of Spanish, he had been assured that the driver he'd reserved would speak English. With so little sleep, he didn't trust that he'd remember how to say *anything* in Spanish.

Within a few minutes, they arrived at Eduardo's black Mercedes sedan and Rob got in the back seat while Eduardo placed the luggage in the trunk. Once behind the wheel, Eduardo turned to Rob. "You are going to the Hotel L17 Metropolitan on Rambla Catalunya, correct?" When Rob nodded, Eduardo continued, "Traffic isn't too bad; we should be there in less than an hour."

Eduardo seemed to sense that Rob wasn't in the mood for chatting, so he remained quiet and listened to music on the radio while he drove. Rob was lost in thought for much of the ride, still dwelling on the fact that he would be experiencing this latest adventure alone and worrying that he'd made a mistake in going through with this trip.

I still miss you so much, Alan. It's been two years, but sometimes it feels like only yesterday when you died. I really wish you were here with me.

Too late to really do anything about the trip now. He'd survive Barcelona and he *knew* he'd feel better once he boarded the cruise ship on Saturday. A week of relaxation and lots of reading on the ship would do him a world of good and once Samantha joined him, she'd keep him from dwelling on the past so much.

"We are here, señor," Eduardo announced. Placing the luggage on the sidewalk, Eduardo said, "Enjoy your stay in Barcelona."

Rob had paid for the car service when he booked it, but he handed Eduardo a tip when he took his bags.

"*Gracias*, Eduardo," he said, then turned and entered the hotel.

Thankfully, there was no line at the front desk when he walked in. The registration area was two ornate wooden desks with comfortable leather chairs for guests checking in.

"*Buenos dias, señor. ¿Puedo servirle?*" the attractive woman behind one of the desks asked as he approached.

"*Si,*" Rob replied. "*¿Hablas inglés?*"

The woman smiled and said "Certainly, may I help you, sir?"

"I'm checking in. I have a reservation under the name Asher."

The woman, whose name tag read 'Isabella' said, "Let me check." She typed into her computer and after a moment said, "Ah yes, you are staying with us for four nights, correct?"

"That's right," Rob said. "Is there any chance that my room is ready?"

Isabella turned back to her computer then replied with a smile, "Yes, I see that your room is available now." Rob breathed a sigh of relief and they quickly completed the check-in process.

Once in his room, Rob kicked off his shoes, set his phone alarm to ring in two hours and climbed onto the king-sized bed. He was asleep within minutes.

CHAPTER 1

Thursday, October 3 – L17 Metropolitan Hotel, Barcelona

Ben Rockingham was restless. He tried napping, but after punching his pillow and turning over a few times, he realized he was too wired to sleep at the moment. He tried to get into the latest book on his Kindle, but reading the same paragraph three times convinced him that he couldn't concentrate enough to read, either.

He'd finished his last interview that morning with a Spanish television talk show, promoting his latest indie film. The movie was set to be released in a few weeks and he'd spent the last couple of weeks in various European cities doing the necessary promo work. He was now taking a little time off—he'd told his agent that it was non-negotiable since he was exhausted—before returning to the US and hitting the talk show circuit prior to the film's debut. When he'd decided to pursue a career as an actor, he never realized that he'd spend so much time promoting his movies. Yes, it needed to be done, but it wasn't something he enjoyed.

He was going to have a serious talk with his agent about cutting back on his schedule a bit. He was fifty-five now and starting to realize that making money wasn't as important to him as it used to be. He'd made enough in the past and wisely invested a good deal of it, so he didn't have to accept every project that came his way. His preference would be to do just a couple of projects a year and take it easy the rest of the time. Life was too short.

Okay, I can't sleep and I can't read, maybe I'll just head down to the bar for a glass of wine or two. He grabbed his phone and his key card and headed downstairs.

AFTER ROAMING the streets in the neighborhood and stopping at one of the sidewalk cafés for lunch, Rob arrived back at his hotel parched and ready for a drink. At four o'clock it was still a sunny sixty-seven degrees, but he was ready for a break, and the hotel bar was just what the doctor ordered. He'd spent some time there over the past couple of days and the eclectic décor, comfortable seating, and relaxed atmosphere suited him just fine.

As he meandered to the bar, he admired the bright orange wall running along one side, filled with random 3-D art pieces and various paintings. He saw a couple sitting on one of the lime green sofas and only one of the eight seats at the bar was occupied by an attractive man who appeared to be around Rob's age.

"Good afternoon, señor Rob," the bartender said as he approached the bar.

"*Buenas tardes,* Carlos. How are you doing today?" Rob asked as he sat at one of the corner bar seats.

"Very good, sir. What can I get you to drink this afternoon?"

Rob thought a moment and then said, "I really enjoyed that Tempranillo you served me yesterday. I'll have another glass of that, please."

Carlos placed the glass of wine in front of Rob and walked away. Rob lifted the glass and made eye contact with the only other patron sitting at the bar. Until now, the man had been focused on his phone, but now he looked at Rob and raised his glass as well.

"*Salud,*" Rob said and took a sip.

"I must agree with you," the stranger said, "the Tempranillo is excellent." He sipped from his own glass.

Rob took a moment to study the man, without obviously staring. He was definitely attractive. While it was hard to judge his height since he was sitting down, Rob guessed he was close to Rob's own six-one. Medium-brown hair falling almost to his shoulders and shot with a bit of gray, piercing green eyes, and a bit of scruff on his cheeks and chin, completed the look of this strikingly handsome man.

Sneaking a quick peek at his throat and the open collar of his dress shirt, Rob spotted a bit of chest hair. But wait, there was something familiar about this man. Rob considered whether he had seen him somewhere before. Then it hit him.

Rob cleared his throat then asked, "Excuse me, but aren't you Ben Rockingham?"

"Yes, I am," the man nodded shyly.

Rob extended his hand, "I'm Rob Asher, it's very nice to meet you. I've seen many of your movies."

They shook hands and Ben said, "It's very nice to meet you, too. What brings you to Barcelona?"

Rob paused. How much should he actually say? This trip was supposed to be about him getting on with his life and trying new things—like spending time in Barcelona and on a cruise ship by himself—this was not the time to bring up the past. But what the heck, he'd never see this guy again. He took a deep breath and smiled.

"I'm actually on vacation. My husband Alan and I planned this trip over two years ago but then Alan suffered a massive coronary several months later. I was going to cancel, but my best friend talked me into doing it anyway. I've spent the last couple of years existing more than living, and Samantha, being the kick-ass BFF that she is, told me it was time to, and I quote, 'Get off my lazy ass and start living again.' So here I am. I've been here for a couple of days and I'm boarding a cruise ship on Saturday."

Realizing he just told a total stranger a whole lot more than was necessary, he quickly added, "I'm sorry if I over-shared a bit there, It's a bad habit of mine."

"I'm very sorry for your loss," Ben said quietly, "but I applaud your resolve to take this trip anyway. That's no small feat. And no apologies necessary."

Rob chuckled, relaxing a bit. "Thank you. Sam *is* a force of nature when she wants to be, so I've learned that it's best to listen to her. It's much safer than suffering her wrath!"

"Yes, I've had a friend or two like that as well, and it's definitely worth listening to them." Ben agreed and then paused a moment before asking, "You said you were boarding a ship on Saturday. May I ask which ship?"

"Sure, the *Ocean Wanderer*," Rob answered. "Why do you ask?"

"Oh, my God!" Ben exclaimed. "I'm getting on the *Ocean Wanderer* on Saturday, too! What a crazy coincidence!"

Rob was shocked and at a loss for what to say next. Part of him had been dreading the first week of the cruise. At least now there'd be one familiar face on board. The thought of spending some time with a handsome man was suddenly quite appealing to him. Yes, he still loved Alan—part of him always would—but Alan would also be the first to kick him in the ass and tell him to enjoy himself.

Trying to appear cool and put-together, Rob said, "Well then, I guess we'll be seeing more of each other."

"Definitely. I'm looking forward to relaxing on the ship for a week. Things have been rather hectic for me lately."

While they were chatting, Carlos managed to catch their eye and held up the bottle of Tempranillo with a questioning look. When they each nodded, Carlos refilled their glasses and moved along. A few more people had wandered into the bar, but it was still relatively quiet.

"Wait a minute, you're only on the ship for a week?" Rob asked.

"Yes, why? Are you cruising longer than that?"

"Three weeks," Rob paused a moment, thinking of the cruise itinerary. "Now I remember. There's a seven-night cruise back to Barcelona first, then there's a two-week sailing with a few more ports in Europe followed by an Atlantic crossing and the ship ends up in Fort Lauderdale. That's where I get off. In fact, my friend Sam is flying here in a week to join me on the cruise for the crossing."

"Well, we'll be on the ship together for a week anyway, so hopefully we can get together for dinner or a drink. Um, if that's something you'd be interested in doing," Ben said.

They'd only just started chatting, but there was something very interesting about this handsome man. Rob wasn't sure what it was yet, but he was definitely interested in spending some time on the cruise with Ben.

"Are you traveling with someone? Not that it's any of my business, but shouldn't you check with them first before you start making plans?" Rob asked.

"No, this is a solo trip for me," Ben replied. "I finished working on an independent film not that long ago and I've been doing a round of interviews about it here in Europe. I've been living out of a suitcase for the past couple of weeks and I don't always remember what city I'm in. I taped my last interview this morning and I'm really looking forward to relaxing for a bit. But then it's back to the States for me."

"Well then, Ben, I'd definitely like to meet for dinner or drinks on the cruise," Rob replied.

"Nice, sounds like we have a plan. And if I'm not being too forward, do you have any plans for dinner tonight? I've got to head back to my room in a few minutes to get on a video call with someone back in California, but I'd really like to continue our chat."

Rob didn't detect anything flirtatious about Ben's question, but he did want to spend more time with him. "No, I've got no plans. I was just going to try a tapas place somewhere in the area, so I'm open to pretty much anything."

"Great. Why don't we meet in the lobby around eight?

There are several great places within a few blocks, so I'm sure we can find something." Ben took a final sip from his glass and rose to leave, extending his hand to Rob.

They sealed the deal with a handshake. "Okay," Rob said. "I'll see you at eight."

As Ben was leaving, he waved at Carlos, calling out, *"Hasta luego, Carlos."*

"¡Hasta luego, mi amigo!" Carlos replied with a grin.

After Ben left, Rob sipped some wine and thought about their conversation. *Was* Ben being a bit flirty? He had no idea.

I'm way out of practice with reading signals. Alan and I were together for twenty years, so I have no idea how to date anymore. Wait, what am I saying? This isn't a date! It's merely two guys who just met and had a short but pleasant conversation who then decided to have dinner together since they're both alone.

The more Rob thought about it, the more he convinced himself he was just overthinking it all. As far as Rob knew, Ben wasn't even gay, but just to be sure he pulled out his phone for a quick Google search. His first instinct had been right—Ben had been married years before. He even had a son who must now be in his late twenties. He was divorced and didn't seem to have any steady love interest.

But something still tickled the back of Rob's mind. *He's not gay, but even if he were, it's too soon after Alan. Although, he is quite attractive!*

Rob shook his head to clear his tumbling thoughts, finished his second glass of wine, and headed back to his room. He was on holiday, and he was bound to meet attractive and interesting people. It didn't mean anything other than that he was getting back into the world again. He couldn't add more meaning to their plan than what it was. It was just dinner, but he needed to rest before that. He'd have time for a quick nap before meeting up with Ben.

BEN PONDERED his conversation with Rob as he made his way back to his room for the video call.

Hmmm, I don't make a habit of noticing attractive guys, but there's something about this guy that's really hard to miss. And it's not just that he's rather handsome. There's something deeper, something below the surface that really excited me while we chatted. I've not felt like this in a very long time—and never this quickly. I need to get to know Rob better. Something tells me this cruise is gonna be lots more than I bargained for!

CHAPTER 2

At five minutes before eight, Rob grabbed his phone and his wallet, checked to make sure his key card was in said wallet, and headed to the door. He stopped suddenly and realized he was a bit nervous.

"Knock it off," he said aloud. "Stop being silly, it's *not* a date!"

Once again shaking his head, he left the room, walked down the hall and pressed the elevator button. When he arrived in the lobby, he looked around, but didn't see Ben. He strolled around a bit, noting the bar crowd had picked up a little, but it didn't seem like it was too much for Carlos to handle.

He turned around, heading toward the front of the hotel and saw Ben getting off the elevator. He waved, then joined him and as they walked through the hotel doors, Ben gestured to the left and said, "There are several good places down this way."

"Sure," Rob agreed. "Even though I've been here before, I don't know much about the city, so any way you suggest will be fine with me."

"I've spent a lot of time in several cities in Spain over the years," Ben replied. "I love Barcelona."

"Alan and I were here a few years ago. We stayed for a couple of days after a transatlantic cruise that started in Florida. On that trip, we visited Sagrada Familia—that was magnificent!"

"Yes, it is beautiful," Ben agreed. "Did you think about going back on this trip?"

"No, I went to Montserrat yesterday instead. The views from up there are phenomenal."

They had been walking for a few minutes when Ben stopped in front of a restaurant. "How's this? I've been here before and the food has always been good. They have a nice bar area—if there's room we can sit there and get some drinks and then order some things to share."

"Sounds good to me."

They entered and Ben spoke to the hostess in fluent Spanish. She led them to two seats at the far end of the bar and left menus with them. Ben turned to Rob, "Do you want some wine? It might make more sense to just get a bottle."

Rob readily agreed, adding, "Order whatever you think is good—I like both red and white."

The bartender walked over, greeting them with a hearty, *"Buenas tardes, señores."*

Ben and the bartender, whose name was Antonio, chatted for a bit and the bartender finally walked away.

"I ordered a bottle of Manto Negro, it's usually a bit lighter than a Tempranillo, thought it might be worth a try. I also ordered some olives and cheese to start us off." Ben told him.

"That sounds great. If they have some of the Catalana tomato bread, I'm definitely interested in that and I'd love some *jamón*, but other than that, I'm open to try just about anything."

Antonio returned with two glasses and the bottle of wine. After opening the wine, he poured a bit into Ben's glass. Ben took a sip, nodded, and Antonio poured wine into each glass. Rob picked up his glass and took a sip, then nodded his approval.

"Wow, this is very good. I think I need to take a photo of the label so I remember it."

He reached for his phone and Ben picked up the bottle and tilted it a bit to give Rob a better shot of the label. Rob snapped a few photos, making sure he got Ben's face in at least one of the photos.

"Thanks. I'll have to look for this when I get home."

"Speaking of home," Ben said, "Where do you hang your hat?"

"Southeastern Massachusetts most of the time...a little town called Westport. But I also have a condo in Florida. How about you? Southern California?"

"I do have a house just outside of LA, but I don't stay there much. There's a family home in England that my brother and I inherited from our parents. I stay there as often as I can. And I've been thinking about getting a cabin somewhere in the

States but haven't yet decided between the Pacific Northwest or New England."

"Well, you can always come to Massachusetts and check out the area if you want, although there is a lot to be said for the Pacific Northwest, too!"

Antonio returned carrying plates laden with an assortment of olives and some cheeses and set them down between the two men.

Ben asked Rob, "Do you like shrimp?"

Rob nodded and Ben turned to the bartender and spoke rapidly in Spanish, although Rob was pretty sure he heard the words for bread and ham.

When Antonio left, Rob said, "I'm glad you speak Spanish so well. My vocabulary is very limited, I usually end up pointing to things on the menu."

"Well, even though I was born in DC, my dad worked for the government and we traveled quite a bit when I was growing up. My mom is English; we lived in both London and Madrid and spent a little bit of time in France, too. I picked up Spanish pretty easily and can get by in French as well."

"I've lived in Massachusetts my whole life. My mom was from Canada, so we did visit relatives there when I was growing up. When Alan and I started seeing each other, we both decided we wanted to travel more, so we took a lot of trips around the US. Once we discovered cruising, we sailed in the Caribbean then expanded our travels to Europe. We did a few land-based trips overseas, but we learned early on that we liked cruising a lot." Rob rubbed a hand over his chest absentmindedly. The ache he felt every time he spoke of Alan was still present but somehow, sitting there with Ben, the pain wasn't quite as sharp as usual.

Antonio delivered more plates of food to them and they continued to chat about all sorts of things. Rob told Ben that he and Alan had been together for twenty years and married for ten of those years. And Rob learned that Ben had been married many years ago but was now divorced and had a twenty-seven-year-old son named Kyle.

"Are you and Kyle close?" Rob asked.

"I think we are. We talk pretty regularly, usually twice a week. Sometimes more, sometimes less, depending on our schedules. He lives in the DC area, but he has been out to LA to visit and he and I have been on vacation together at the house in England. I think he turned out pretty well."

Rob was curious to know more. "What does he do?"

"He works in finance. He was always interested in math and numbers—God knows he didn't get that from me—and he landed a job at a fairly-large bank when he finished college. He's planning on going on for his masters, but the bank will help him continue his education."

"That's great! Alan was a finance guy, too. He worked for a financial planning firm for a number of years. I, on the other hand, can barely manage to balance my checkbook."

"What do you do, Rob?" he asked.

"I'm a graphic designer. I was working for a major toy and game company that's based in Rhode Island. I was doing mostly package design for them, but now I'm actually retired."

"Retired?" Ben said, surprised. "You don't look old enough to be retired."

"Technically, I'm not. I turned fifty-eight in July, but about five years ago, Alan and I hit the lottery—literally. We won a jackpot in a multi-state lottery. After taxes, we still ended up with several million dollars."

"Wow. I don't think I've ever met someone who hit the lottery for a major prize like that. It must have been a crazy time for you when it happened."

"Yeah, it was mind-boggling and quite overwhelming. The weird thing is, we weren't even regular players. Every once in a while, one of us—frankly it was usually me— would buy a ticket, typically when the jackpot was getting quite large. That particular week, we were dining out at a local favorite restaurant and I noticed that the jackpot was huge, so I impulsively bought five quick-pick tickets."

Rob stopped for a moment, shaking his head, "I still can't believe we won. It was Sunday morning and Alan had to remind me to check my ticket. I opened the lottery app on my phone and I couldn't stop shaking when I realized we had the winning numbers."

"That's amazing!" Ben declared. "What did you do next?"

"After triple-checking that we did, in fact, have the winning numbers, we signed the back of the ticket and put it in our safe so that nothing would happen to it. We talked about some things we wanted to do, like give some of the money to charity and also help out some family and friends. Alan did some research about how much we should donate, how we could best invest some of the money, and we talked to our lawyer about it so that everything was handled correctly. We also waited to see if there were any other winners. I wanted to go to the lottery office right away, but Alan explained waiting would give us time to make some decisions plus we'd know exactly how much we'd won. It took about a month before we had worked out all the details of what we wanted to do. At that point, we knew there were no other jackpot winners, so we went to the lottery office and turned in our ticket."

"Did you both retire right away?"

"Yeah, we did. We figured we were young enough to enjoy ourselves and travel like we wanted. With Alan's knowledge of the financial world, he was able to make some wise investments so we wouldn't have to worry about money ever again. We did donate to the local food bank and to the Trevor Project, and as I mentioned, we did help out a few people in our lives who had been struggling a bit. Even though I officially retired, I still dabble in design a bit. I have some friends who have small businesses, so I've helped them with packaging, logos, menu designs, and all sorts of other things. I really enjoy design, so I want to keep doing what I can. Plus, I think I'd go stir-crazy if I didn't have something to do most days. But I make sure my schedule is flexible enough that I can travel when I want."

He paused briefly, then added, "Even if I haven't been doing a lot of that lately. It's just been so difficult for me to even think about traveling alone. I'm not convinced that I'm cut out for it. But I promised Sam that I'd try, so here I am."

Ben beamed at him and nodded approvingly. "What you've been able to do because of winning the lottery is fantastic. It's good that you have things to keep you busy and hopefully now that you've started traveling again, as difficult as that might seem now, you'll do more; I'm sure of it since you seem to enjoy it so much."

Rob smiled. "Yes, I do love visiting new places. This trip really is a test—can I travel on my own and have a good time? Am I willing to put myself out there and meet new people and experience new things? Sure, I built in a little cushion by having Sam join me in a week so that if I don't fare so well, she'll be there to catch me and convince me I'm not broken. But so far, it's been a lot better than I had hoped."

Ben grinned again. "I'm glad things are going well for you so far; I hope that continues. For what it's worth, I don't think you're broken. You're dealing with some new challenges, but you seem to be coping well."

"Thanks for saying that, Ben. I know we just met, but you're very easy to talk to and you've helped keep my mind on other things. I appreciate it."

"No problem. And just so you understand, it goes both ways. As much as I was looking forward to having some quiet time to relax, I didn't want to isolate myself completely. I'm glad we're able to spend some time together."

They continued to chat about various topics, but all too soon their plates of food and bottle of wine were empty. Rob tried to object when Ben insisted on paying for the meal, but he was quickly silenced, "I invited you to join me, so that's that," Ben said with a cheeky grin.

Once again, the wheels in Rob's brain started turning. Was this a date? It partly felt like one, but on the other hand, nothing Ben did or said seemed at all like he was trying to flirt. It was all so confusing to Rob. He felt like a fish out of water, since he'd been out of the dating pool for so long. He decided he wasn't going to dwell on it anymore as they got up and headed back toward the hotel.

"Do you have anything special planned for tomorrow, Rob?"

"Not really. I'll probably just wander the neighborhood

again and maybe do a bit of window-shopping. What are you doing?"

Sidestepping a couple walking in the opposite direction, Ben said, "I've actually booked an appointment at a spa for a good part of the day. It's a place I've been to before. They have a series of mineral pools you can soak in plus massages, facials, sauna. It's a really great place and they have a special package for a full treatment."

Rob's eyes widened. "Oh my God, that sounds amazing! Any chance I can intrude a bit and join you? I'd love to get an appointment for a massage, but I could use your help as an interpreter."

Ben smiled as he replied, "Of course. In fact, let's meet for breakfast and I'll call the spa when they open to see if they can fit you in. If you decide you want to try the pools or sauna, you'll need a bathing suit."

"Thanks, that sounds great. What time do you want to meet for breakfast?"

"Let's say eight-thirty. I believe the spa opens at nine, so we can grab a bite to eat and then I'll call. My appointment is at ten o'clock, but it's only about ten minutes by cab to the place."

As they approached the hotel, Rob said "Seeing as you bought me dinner, would you like to join me in the bar for a nightcap?"

"Sure," Ben replied.

They entered the hotel and proceeded directly to the bar. There were people at a couple of the sofas and chairs, and three people at the bar, so they headed to the corner of the bar where they could each sit at an end making it easier to chat.

"*Buenas tardes, señores*,' Carlos greeted them. "What can I get you to drink?"

"Do you have any American whiskey, like a nice bourbon?" Rob asked.

"*Si*, I have Maker's Mark and Woodford Reserve."

"I'll have Woodford Reserve on the rocks, please," Rob replied.

"I'll have the same," Ben added.

Carlos quickly poured two generous servings and set the glasses before them. "Enjoy." Then he moved away to take care of another customer.

Ben lifted his glass. "Cheers!"

Rob clinked his glass with Ben's then took a sip. "Ah," he said, "that's good."

"That it is," Ben agreed.

"So, I feel like I'm monopolizing your time," Rob confessed. "We hung out at the bar earlier, had dinner together, and now we've made plans for tomorrow. If I'm making a pest of myself, feel free to tell me to get lost."

"Don't be ridiculous!" Ben replied. "You're not a pest at all. I've enjoyed the time we've spent together, and I look forward to spending more time with you on the cruise, if you still want to. You're a nice guy, easygoing; we've had some interesting conversations."

"Whew, okay, good," Rob answered, feeling very relieved and a little excited. "I've already told you I haven't really traveled since Alan passed away, and I'm feeling a bit nervous about doing things on my own. It's been pretty easy with you and I didn't want to take advantage."

"No worries, Rob. We're good. In fact, while we're on the cruise, you can decide how much, or how little, time we spend together. I have no plans at all, other than to finish the book I'm reading and maybe start another. If you want to hang out, let me know. If you want some alone time, that's fine, too. But I understand that you're a little nervous about traveling alone, so if you need someone to hang out with, I'm happy to spend time with you."

"Thanks, Ben, I really appreciate that."

They sipped their drinks before Ben said, "I must confess, while I've cruised before, it's been a while and I'm sorely out of practice. I'll need to pick your brain about things, if that's okay?"

"Absolutely, Ben! In fact, we can talk about a few things tomorrow so you're ready to board the ship on Saturday, alright?"

"Yes, that's a really good idea."

They finished their drinks and Rob asked Carlos to add the tab to his hotel bill, then left him a tip on the bar. They headed to the elevator and both reached for the button marked '4.' Ben got there first and as he pressed it, they both chuckled.

"Looks like we're neighbors," Rob commented.

As they stepped off the elevator, Ben turned to the left and Rob to the right. Ben looked at Rob and said, "Good night, Rob. See you in the morning."

ROB GOT to his room and thought about the evening as he undressed and brushed his teeth. Parts of it definitely felt like a date, but again, no flirting on Ben's part and he wasn't really feeling a gay vibe from him, either. Nothing he had seen online gave any indication that Ben might be bi, so maybe he was over-analyzing again.

Alan used to tell him that he thought way too hard about so many things. Ah well, he really wasn't looking for romance, anyway. But finding a new friend? Yeah, that seemed like a real possibility here. Ben was a great guy. He was low-key and down-to-earth. He didn't come across as a 'movie star' and Rob really liked that. Ben could definitely become a good friend if that was something he wanted.

He set an alarm and got under the covers, wondering if he'd have any trouble falling asleep. Since Alan's death, sleep hadn't always come easy to Rob. He missed having someone lying next to him, even though Alan's snoring sometimes meant that he had to go to the guest room in order to get some rest. He was thinking of Ben and how nice he was as he drifted off to sleep.

CHAPTER 3

Ben rolled over and looked at the clock on the nightstand. The alarm on his phone would go off in fifteen minutes. Just enough time to lie there and think about yesterday. Meeting Rob at the bar had been a pleasant surprise. And though Rob recognized him right away, he didn't act like he was an over-the-top fan who only wanted to chat with Ben for bragging rights later. He just seemed like an all-around nice guy.

Rob was handsome, but there was more to it than just his good looks. Sure, Ben had always found both men and women attractive, but no man had put butterflies in his stomach since Ryan back in college. Until now. Fuck, was there any chance that Rob maybe felt the same way? Yes, he was gay, but his husband died two years ago and he was obviously still in mourning; only natural considering how long they had been together.

What do I know? I haven't had feelings like this for such a long time—wait, do I have feelings for Rob?

Something is definitely going on here, but I'm not really sure what. Ryan was a great boyfriend, but it was the '80s then and we had hidden our feelings from pretty much everyone. We'd known each other for years and just kind of fell into a romance after admitting that we found each other attractive. At the time, there was so much homophobia out there and neither one of us had been ready to be out and proud. Over time, we had drifted apart and then I met Caroline. And while we got along great at the beginning, our relationship had mostly been rocky, if I was being honest. We did have Kyle though, so it hadn't been all bad.

"Okay," he said aloud, "I had a short relationship with a guy thirty-plus years ago and then a longer relationship and marriage with a woman a few years after that, and not much of anything since then." He paused a moment, trying to organize his thoughts. "Both of those relationships had taken a while to develop. I'd never experienced 'love at first sight' or 'lust at first sight' or whatever the hell this was. Sure, a few dates here and there, but nothing that really felt completely right. For so many years I thought that either I was bi or that Ryan was just a one-time thing."

But now, after spending just a few hours with Rob, he's all I can think about.

Ben remembered a movie set he had been on a few years ago. He'd been chatting with one of the crew one day and the guy mentioned that he was 'demi.'

"Demi? What the hell is that?" Ben had wanted to know.

"Demisexual," the guy had replied. "I like girls and I like

guys, but unless I have an emotional connection to them, I can't get serious. Casual sex just doesn't do it for me, but if we connect emotionally, it's magical."

That had stuck in the back of Ben's mind and sometimes he thought that maybe he was demisexual too. He had done a bit of research at one point and it seemed like the emotional connection took a bit of time to develop. That certainly fit in with what he'd experienced before. It had been so long since he felt anything for anyone, he had started to think maybe he was asexual. Now, those emotions were starting to stir again when he thought of Rob. Was this really happening?

Ben's phone began to chime, so he reached over and shut off the alarm, then got up and began to get ready for the new day.

***

Rob's alarm woke him. He couldn't believe he'd slept all the way through the night. He hadn't even got up to pee at three in the morning like he often did, no small feat for someone his age. Parts of a dream floated to the surface of his mind. He was with Ben; they were on the ship, out on the balcony of his suite, and they were kissing...

Stop that! Why was he dreaming about kissing Ben? Okay, he did find him attractive, but they'd just met; he was pretty sure the guy wasn't having thoughts about kissing him.

Okay, get your ass in gear so that you're not late for breakfast.

After his much-needed pee, he shaved, showered, and dressed in a pair of chinos and a long-sleeved navy-blue Henley. Checking his watch, he realized he still had time before he was to meet Ben, so he texted Sam. He knew she wouldn't see it for several hours, but he wanted her to know he was thinking about her.

> Hey, Sam! How R U? Guess who I met at the
> hotel bar yesterday? (think hot actor!) My lips
> are sealed! CU next week!

Ha, that'll drive her crazy for sure! He grabbed his phone and wallet and headed out the door. As he neared the elevator, he saw Ben walking toward him from the other end of the hall. Rob noticed how great Ben looked in jeans and a lightweight sweater in sage green, the color made his eyes sparkle.

"Good morning, Ben."

"Hi, Rob. How are you doing today?"

Rob hit the elevator button. "I'm fine, slept really well last night. I didn't wake up until my alarm rang."

The elevator door opened and thankfully, it was empty. The cars were so tiny they didn't easily fit more than two or three people. They got in and headed down to the lobby.

As they walked to the breakfast buffet area, Rob asked, "And how did you sleep?"

"I slept well. I did wake up at one point, but I was able to quickly fall back to sleep."

The buffet area was a bit busy, but there were a few tables available, so they picked one and a server came over with a carafe of coffee. Putting it in the center of the table, they asked, "Do you need tea or decaf?"

Both men answered in the negative and the server moved away to take care of another table. Ben poured coffee for both of them, and those first sips had them both sighing. Then they stood and made their way to the food.

"There's nothing like that first sip," Ben declared.

Rob agreed, "Amen to that."

There was a short line, while they waited Ben said, "I don't know what you usually eat for breakfast, but I'm going to go easy this morning. I need a little bit of something, but don't like to eat too heavy before a massage."

"That makes a lot of sense. I'll do the same, thanks."

They each grabbed some fresh fruit and yogurt; Rob snagged a chocolate croissant while Ben opted for a lemon danish. They returned to their table and began eating.

Rob pondered for a moment before saying, "You mentioned that you got a special package deal at the spa. What does the package include and just out of curiosity, how much does it cost?"

"It includes a one-hour massage and a thirty-minute facial along with self-paced use of the mineral-spring pools and saunas. The last time I did something like this, I was there for a little over three hours. I did the massage first, followed by the facial. Then you can relax and take your time moving between the pools and sauna. The package price was one hundred forty-nine euros."

Rob looked surprised, "That's an amazing deal. It's what I would expect to pay for only a massage. I think I'd like to get the package too, if they still have availability."

Ben grinned. "Yeah, over the years I've found that many European cities have some great spas that aren't outrageously priced like they can be in the States. There are certainly places that cost more, but why pay more when you don't have to?"

"I couldn't agree more."

Once they had both finished eating and were enjoying a second cup of coffee, the server stopped by to ask if they needed anything else. Ben and Rob each handed over a card they had received at check-in—this confirmed that breakfast was included with the room.

Ben glanced at his watch and said, "It's five minutes past nine. I'm going to call the spa now."

They rose and walked to a quiet corner of the lobby where Ben pulled out his phone, searched for a number, and dialed. As he spoke, Rob thought he caught the words 'friend' and 'reservation,' but that was really all he could understand.

Still on the phone, Ben said, *"Sí, gracias."* He looked at Rob, smiled and gave him a thumbs-up.

"Gracias, hasta luego." Ben ended the call and said to Rob, "You're all set. I was able to get the same package that I have. And someone called yesterday afternoon to cancel a massage this morning, so your massage will be at ten o'clock, too."

"Excellent. Thank you so much, Ben. I really appreciate it."

"No problem. I'm glad it's all working out. I'm going to go to my room and grab my stuff." He checked his watch, "Do you want to meet back here in about twenty minutes?"

Rob looked at the time on his phone and said, "Sure. You said I just need a bathing suit, right?"

They started walking toward the elevator. "Yes," said Ben. "If you have a pair of flip-flops, bring those, too. But if you don't, they have some disposable ones at the spa. And the locker rooms have soap, shampoo and towels, so you don't need to worry about any of that."

They got off the elevator and headed to their rooms. "See you shortly," Rob said.

Once in his room, Ben brushed his teeth and thought back to breakfast. Rob was definitely pushing all the right buttons for him. His Henley really made his blue eyes brighter and as he followed Rob into the restaurant, he'd taken the opportunity to check out his ass in those tight chinos and he definitely liked what he saw.

Well, we're going to a spa together, so hopefully I'll get to see a bit more of him.

With that happy thought, he grabbed his flip-flops and bathing suit, tossing them into his backpack. He paused and thought a moment, then added his Kindle. He didn't know if he'd have time to read, but better safe than sorry.

He checked his phone messages, but there were no texts and just a couple of emails that he quickly deleted. Grabbing his backpack, he headed out the door and down to the lobby.

Ben didn't see Rob anywhere in the lobby, so he sat in a chair which would allow him to keep an eye on the elevator door while he waited.

Rob's bathing suit was already tightly stuffed into a ziplock bag, so he tucked it and his flip-flops into the mini-backpack that held his AirPods and Kindle. He never went anywhere without that bag.

After brushing his teeth and using the facilities, Rob stepped off the elevator ready for a day of relaxation and fun with Ben. His date—or not date—was sitting in the lobby waiting for him with a big grin on his handsome face. And it was aimed straight at Rob.

Oh my God, his eyes really light up when he smiles. Could he be any more handsome?

"Ready to go?" Rob asked aloud, ignoring his thoughts.

"Yeah."

As they walked out the door Ben looked around for a taxi. "This is a busy neighborhood so finding a cab shouldn't be difficult," he said.

Just then, a taxi pulled up in front of the hotel and a passenger exited from the back seat. Ben caught the driver's eye and pointed at himself and Rob with a questioning look. The driver nodded and they got in. The driver turned to Ben and said, "Excuse me, señor, but aren't you Ben Rockingham?"

"Yes, I am." Ben responded, anticipating what was coming next.

"If it's not too much trouble, may I have your autograph, *por favor?*"

"Of course. It's no problem at all." Ben signed the paper that the driver handed him, gave him the address to the spa, and then sat back for the short ride.

"*Muchos gracias*, señor."

When they arrived, Rob paid the taxi driver. Once they'd exited the cab, Rob asked, "Does that happen very often? The autograph, I mean."

"Not too often, but enough and I really don't mind. They say you need to worry when fans *stop* asking for your autograph." Ben chuckled at his own joke. "And truly, I don't get noticed as much as many other actors, so I'm fine with it."

From the outside, the building where the spa was located looked ancient, but once inside, Rob could see that the old structure had been artfully combined with sleek modern design to create a beautiful and relaxing space. Ben spoke to someone at the reception desk and then turned to Rob.

"They'll need your credit card now for the cost of the package. You can give the individual therapists a gratuity in euros or by credit card separately after each treatment."

Rob handed over his card, signed where indicated, and said, "*Gracias.*"

The receptionist handed each of them a key on an elastic wristband and pointed toward the changing rooms. Using the number stamped on the keys, they located their lockers and began to undress.

"Just wrap a towel around your waist for now," Ben explained, indicating a stack of towels at the end of the row of lockers. Wearing only his black boxer briefs, he walked over to the towels and picked up two of them. Rob couldn't help but admire Ben's hairy chest and the dark trail that disappeared below the waistband of his briefs. Ben handed him a towel.

Rob said, "Thanks," and turned away, silently doing multiplication tables in his head and praying that he wouldn't pop a boner right then. The sight of Ben's body was more than a little appealing.

"There's a waiting area through that other doorway," Ben said, pointing to a doorway on the opposite side of the changing room from where they had entered. "They'll come for us there for our massages. After that, come back here and shower and put your suit on. Then head back to the waiting area and someone will get you for your facial. Later, we can check out the pools and sauna."

Towels securely in place, they headed to the waiting area to wait for their first treatment.

AFTER HIS MASSAGE, Ben went to the changing room, grabbed a fresh towel, and threw his used one into a bin near the showers. The shower room had semi-private stalls on two walls, with half-high glass-block dividers separating each of the eight showers. The third wall had a row of hooks, so Ben hung his towel on a hook and went to one of the showers.

He used the shampoo and body wash in the wall dispensers to wash all the massage oil off. The oil felt good going on, but it felt really good to wash it off.

He thought back to earlier in the locker room when they were both getting undressed, and he'd caught a glimpse of Rob's naked ass as he slipped off his gray underwear.

Just as nice as I suspected. Damn, he looks good. Shit, what am I doing? I shouldn't be thinking things like that. It's way too soon.

He turned to rinse off his back and saw Rob enter the shower room. He pointed to the bin for used towels and said, "You can toss your used towel in there and grab a clean one from the pile."

Rob smiled back and muttered, "Thanks," as he shed his towel and dropped it in the bin. He grabbed a new one and, placing it on a hook, hurried to one of the showers.

Ben couldn't get over the sight of Rob as the other man shucked his towel and moved to a shower. Even though he was a few years older than him, Rob clearly worked out. Firm stomach, broad chest with a smattering of hair which trailed down below his navel to a nice thatch of pubic hair. He took a quick look but didn't linger. One didn't stare at another guy's junk in the locker room.

Ben turned, dialing down the temperature of the water to

try and keep his cock from paying too much attention to Rob. He rinsed off quickly, grabbed his towel and dried off, then headed back to his locker for his bathing suit.

Rob arrived just a couple of minutes later, freshly showered and grinning. "Oh my God, that massage was amazing!"

He unlocked his locker, grabbed his swimsuit and pulled it on. The guys tossed their wet towels into the used towel bin and headed to the waiting area.

WHILE HE WAITED for his facial, Rob's mind wandered back to the sight of Ben in the shower.

Fuck, he's gorgeous!

He'd tried not to stare, but only half succeeded. It was apparent that Ben didn't do any manscaping, and that was definitely a turn-on for Rob. He hadn't trusted his dick to behave in front of Ben, but he didn't think Ben had noticed anything out of the ordinary. Luckily, reciting the Fibonacci Sequence in his head kept things under control while he showered. *Zero, one, one, two, three, five, eight, thirteen, twenty-one...*

CHAPTER 4

After a second shower and exhilarating facial, Rob and Ben took a long soak in each of the three mineral pools then sat for a while in the sauna. It had been the best day and Rob was truly grateful.

"Thank you for letting me tag along on your spa day. It was amazing and I haven't felt so relaxed in a long time," he told Ben as they dressed to leave.

"No problem," Ben replied. "I enjoyed it too." He checked his watch and continued, "It's been almost five hours since breakfast. If I remember correctly, there's a café a couple of doors down. Do you want to grab some lunch?"

"Yeah, I definitely could eat."

They left the spa and walked to the café down the block.

Once seated, Ben looked over the menu and said, "In the spirit of having a healthy spa day, I think I'll get a salad with some grilled chicken."

"A salad sounds great, but I think I'd rather have it with marinated shrimp," Rob replied.

While they waited for their food, they each checked their phones and after a moment, Rob laughed.

"What's so funny?"

"Oh, I texted Sam this morning before breakfast and told her I met an actor at the hotel yesterday. I didn't tell her your name so now she's bugging me to find out who you are."

Ben chuckled, "Are you gonna keep her in suspense for a week? I don't mind if you tell her who I am. She's not likely to call a magazine and sic the paparazzi on me, right?"

"Not at all," Rob assured him. "She's many things, but trustworthy and loyal are at the top of the list. Let me reply to her now, or she'll be bugging me all day."

> Calm down, Sam! OK, I'll tell U - it's Ben
> Rockingham. We R having lunch right now.
> I'll call U later.

"There, that should hold her for now," Rob said, setting his phone aside.

"What does Sam do, Rob?"

"She's a travel agent. That's how we met."

He paused as the server arrived with their food, along with a bottle of sparkling water that Ben had ordered. After admiring his meal and taking the first bite, Rob continued.

"Wow, it's gotta be seventeen or eighteen years now. Alan and I were talking about doing a cruise for the first time and decided to use a travel agent since we knew next to nothing about cruises at that point. We found a local agency advertising that they specialized in cruises, and we stopped by their office to pick up a brochure or two. We met Sam that day and she helped us figure out where we wanted to go and what our best cruise options were. She did such a great job with the first one, we went back to her the next time we wanted to travel. Over time, we got friendlier and now, she's family."

Rob smiled thoughtfully, thinking fondly of his friend, and added, "In fact, after Alan and I hit the lottery, Sam is one of the people that we helped. She really wasn't happy with the agency where she was working, so we gave her a bit of seed money so that she could start up her own agency. It's called Wanderlust Travel and is doing so well, she now has a few agents working for her, along with a customer service rep.

"That's wonderful," Ben replied. "It's so nice that you were able to help her out like that."

"Like I mentioned earlier, she's family." Rob said. "She's got a few cousins and an aunt in Arizona, but she doesn't see them all that often. She was dating a guy several years ago, I think they had been together for about five years or so. But he turned out to be a real jerk, so she dumped him."

Rob took another bite of salad then continued, "She's so much happier and carefree now. And she's fiercely loyal to her friends. She comes across as overprotective sometimes, but I think it's because she has a huge heart and wants to take care of people."

Ben thought for a moment and then asked, "She sounds wonderful and I'm glad you have each other. You say she's family, do you have any other family? Brothers, sisters?"

"Yeah, I have a brother and a sister. Technically, they're

stepsiblings. My dad remarried after my mom passed away fifteen years ago and his wife had two children from her first marriage. But we became very close, and I truly think of them as just my brother and sister. Geoff is my age and Megan is two years younger. Our parents are all gone now, but we've stayed close." He turned curious eyes to Ben, "What about you, Ben? Any brothers or sisters?

"An older brother. Michael will be sixty in January. He's a lawyer in DC."

As they finished their meal, Rob said, "I told Sam that I would call her this afternoon and then I think I'm going to take a nap. But since you were kind enough to buy me dinner last night, can I return the favor tonight? That is, if you don't have other plans."

Ben smiled. "I don't have any other plans and I'd love to join you for dinner tonight. I'm probably gonna nap this afternoon, too. Getting a massage always has that effect on me."

He thought for a moment and then said, "Why don't we meet at the hotel bar around six-thirty? We can have a drink and then figure out where we want to go for dinner."

They settled up the bill for lunch and Ben hailed a cab to take them to the hotel.

BACK IN HIS ROOM, Ben hung his bathing suit over the shower rod in the bathroom to dry, then put his Kindle on the nightstand. He undressed, set an alarm on his phone for five-thirty and got into bed. He decided to read for a bit and powered up his Kindle. He was about halfway into the latest book in his favorite cozy mystery series, and he was desperately trying to figure out who the killer was.

He'd only read for a few minutes when his eyes started to close. *No point in fighting it.* He shut off the Kindle, turned on his side, and fell asleep thinking about how much he enjoyed Rob's company.

———

Rob hung up his swimsuit as soon as he got back to his room. It would dry in plenty of time for him to repack it before leaving for the cruise terminal in the morning, but if not, well that's why he carried ziplock bags with him when he traveled.

He sat on the loveseat in the corner. Looking around the room, he was glad they'd picked this hotel when they made plans for this trip. While the other L17 hotels he and Alan had stayed at were all nice, this was the best so far. With its wood-laminate floors and sleek, modern king-sized bed topped off with a snowy white duvet, it was modern and stylish, but the teal upholstered loveseat with bright orange and lime pillows made it feel warm and comfortable.

He checked his phone and saw that Sam had texted him several times, not happy that he hadn't responded to her endless questions about Ben.

He smiled and shook his head. *She's relentless, but I love her. I know she just wants me to be happy, but she doesn't have to get all mama bear on me all the time,* he thought as he called her by tapping her name in his favorites list.

"Finally," Sam said when she answered the phone. "I'm dying here. How the hell did you meet Ben Rockingham?"

"It was totally by accident, Sam. I spent a good part of

yesterday walking around the neighborhood near the hotel. It's really a nice area with lots of little shops and restaurants.

"After lunch, I came back to the hotel and was in my room thinking about either reading or taking a nap and I thought, 'If Sam were here, she'd tell me to go to the bar, have a drink, and live a little.' So I took that advice and went down to the hotel bar. Lo and behold, Ben was sitting there having a glass of wine. We started chatting and that turned into having dinner together."

"First of all," Sam said, "You bet your ass I would tell you to go to the bar and have some fun. That's what this trip is about, right?"

Without giving him a chance to respond, she barreled on, "And exactly who are you and what have you done with the real Rob Asher? 'Cause the guy I know wouldn't be chatting up a hot actor in a bar in Barcelona." She laughed and went on, "Seriously though, I'm super proud of you for doing what you did, sweetie. I know it wasn't easy."

Rob chuckled at what he thought of as Sam's reply behavior. Make a joke and then let him know that she cared. "No, it wasn't easy, but it felt good, Sam. Really good."

"Oh Rob, I'm really happy for you. So, drinks and dinner last night and now lunch today with him. I don't recall ever reading anything about him being into guys, so I'm not gonna assume that you're thinking about dating or anything, so what's going on?"

"Damned if I know Sam," Rob replied. "I'm not getting any kind of vibe from him, but maybe my gaydar is on the fritz. He's very nice and easy to talk to. He's not all *'I'm a famous actor and you should be in awe of me.'* He's just a regular guy and I really enjoy hanging out with him. We went to a really nice tapas place a few blocks from here last night and in the course of conversation he mentioned he was going to a spa this morning for a massage and to soak in their mineral pools. I was feeling a bit braver than usual, so I asked him if I could go with him since I could really use a massage."

Rob paused for a moment, remembering what a nice day he'd had and how accommodating Ben had been.

"He said sure and even offered to call the spa this morning to see if I could get an appointment. Plus, he's fluent in Spanish so that was a huge help to me. Anyway, the massage was amazing, and we had just arrived at a café near the spa when I saw your message. It would have been rude to call you at that moment, so I made you wait."

"Okay, since you were having lunch with Ben Rocking-ham, I forgive you," Sam proclaimed, dramatically. Rob laughed. He knew she was just giving him a hard time and really wasn't upset that she had to wait to hear from him. "And he speaks Spanish fluently? How sexy is that? But seri-ously," she continued, "I just want you to be happy. Damn, if I were there, I'd be able to figure him out in a heartbeat."

"You sure as hell would," Rob agreed. "And yes, I know you want me to be happy."

Rob paused and took a deep breath, "Okay, I'm feeling something for sure, I'm just not sure what yet. He knows I'm gay, but maybe he's just not feeling what I'm feeling, even though I have no idea what I'm feeling." He paused, then added, chagrined, "Oh my God, I'm rambling, aren't I Sam? Besides, it's too soon. Alan hasn't been gone that long and I shouldn't be looking at other guys and thinking..." he trailed off guiltily.

"Yes, you're rambling, and Alan would be the first one to

kick your ass and tell you to go for it and… wait, what *are* you thinking?"

Rob shook his head, smiling—of course Sam picked up on the fact he was thinking something…

"You're gonna think I'm silly, but I'm thinking that I might wanna kiss him and I wouldn't mind if he maybe kissed me back," he replied, his tone softening. Sam could probably tell that he was blushing a bit as he said it.

"I don't think you're silly, Rob. I think that's fantastic! But you get on the ship tomorrow so you only have today. Why are you talking to me when you could be kissing that hunk?"

"Actually," Rob confessed, "we're having dinner tonight. Not that I have the guts to actually kiss the guy when I don't even know if he likes guys. But I haven't told you the best part yet."

"Tell me the hotel gave away his room by mistake and he's gonna have to bunk with you tonight?" Sam asked expectantly.

A bark of laughter burst from Rob's lips. "Don't be ridiculous, Sam. What I haven't told you yet is that Ben is gonna be on the cruise for the first week, so we'll spend a bit more time together."

"Get the fuck outta here, Rob!" Sam exclaimed, "That's awesome. You'll have a week to make your move, but don't wait too long. I know they sell condoms in the gift shop on the ship, lube too, I bet. Be sure to pick some up as soon as it opens the first day. That way you'll be prepared."

Rob knew it was just best to agree with her at times like this. "Sure, Sam. Fine, Sam. Will do, Sam." But he had no plans of walking into the ship's gift shop to buy condoms or lube.

"Listen," he continued, "I want to take a little nap before I meet Ben in the bar for drinks later, so I'm gonna say goodbye now, sweetie. I'll see you in a week. Love you!"

"Love you, too, Rob! And remember, I want to know everything that happened between the two of you, so be ready to tell me when I see you in a week!" And with that, she ended the call.

Rob set an alarm on his phone, quickly undressed, and slipped under the covers. He fell asleep thinking about kissing Ben.

BEN SAT at the bar sipping a glass of Tempranillo. Carlos had actually held up the bottle when he saw Ben approaching the bar. When he nodded, Carlos poured a glass. By the time Ben got to the bar, the glass was waiting for him.

Rob wasn't there yet, but Ben had arrived a few minutes early. He planned it that way so he could examine how he was feeling. As he swirled the wine in his glass he thought of Rob. It had only been natural for him to get undressed at the spa, so he'd been expecting that. What he hadn't anticipated was his reaction to it. It had excited him. If he hadn't turned around and adjusted the water temperature in the shower, Rob would have seen more than he bargained for, or at least more than Ben intended.

Yes, he had feelings for Rob. But did he want to act on them? What if Rob didn't feel the same way? Something about Rob felt special and Ben didn't want to hurt him. Damn it. Why was this so difficult?

Okay, maybe if an opportunity presents itself, I'll say something. If I don't chicken out that is.

A few minutes later, Rob walked into the bar and sat down next to Ben. He gave Ben a smile then looked at Carlos and said, "I'll have what he's having."

Ben laughed and teased, "You sound pretty sure of yourself. What if I'm drinking something awful?"

"Nah, you seem to have pretty good taste, so I'm willing to take my chances."

Carlos set a glass of red wine in front of him. Lifting it, Rob said, "Cheers!"

Ben smiled at him and raised his own glass to clink against Rob's.

Rob sipped the wine and declared, "I was right. It's perfect."

Just like you, thought Ben.

Rob broke into Ben's reverie. "Did you take a nap?"

"Yeah," Ben said, a little flustered. "I tried to read but only got through about a page when my eyes started to close. So I gave up on reading and just slept. What about you?"

"I called Sam and chatted with her for a while and then yeah, I napped too."

"How is Sam doing? Did she badger you for information about me?" Ben had a bit of a devious look on his face when he asked his question.

"Shit, it's like you know her! Are you two ganging up on me?" Rob grinned, enjoying the banter. "Actually, she thinks it's great that I met someone to chat with and is jealous that she's not here to badger you herself."

Ben laughed, "She sounds like quite a character. I'm sorry I won't get to meet her."

"Well, I have a week to convince you to pay me a visit in Massachusetts sometime. You'd meet her for sure then." Rob was a bit surprised at himself for being so bold, but it felt right so he went with it.

"I would definitely consider that," Ben admitted, "especially if it meant meeting Sam. I imagine the two of you together are probably quite a pair. Although, you're gay, right Rob? So you're not like a 'pair' are you?" Ben asked, putting air quotes around pair as he spoke.

"No, we're definitely not that kind of pair. She's really more my sister than anything else." Rob looked at him thoughtfully. A visit from Ben would be great, and he and Sam would definitely get along. "We'll have to make plans for that, then."

Switching subjects, Ben asked, "Do you have any thoughts about dinner tonight? Something similar to last night, or are you wanting a bit more?"

Oh, I definitely want more, Ben. Lots more, Rob thought. Out loud he said, "I think a larger meal tonight is in order. I mean, we didn't have much for breakfast and just a salad for lunch."

"Yes, that's true," Ben agreed. "Would you be interested in seafood?"

"Definitely. But I wouldn't object if they also had some *jamón* as an appetizer," Rob said, with a twinkle in his eye.

Ben laughed, "I agree! I think I know just the place."

He called Carlos over and they exchanged a few words. Then Carlos headed to the phone located at the other end of the bar to make a call.

He returned a few minutes later and said, "You are all set,

señor Ben. You have a reservation for two at eight-thirty this evening."

"*Gracias*, Carlos."

Ben turned to Rob, "I haven't been to this place for a while but last time I was there, it was wonderful, and Carlos agreed that it's still great. It's near the water and we'll need to take a cab there, but we have a bit of time before we need to leave. Do you want another glass of wine and we can talk about cruises?"

"Yes, please."

Ben caught the attention of Carlos and pointed at the two now-empty glasses. Carlos nodded and quickly refilled them.

"So," Rob began, "how long has it been since you were last on a cruise, Ben?"

"About five or six years, I think. It was a seven-day cruise in the Caribbean with my brother and his family."

"Okay, so a few things may have changed, but not much. Have you downloaded the cruise line's app to your phone yet?"

"Yes, I downloaded it a few days ago, but I can't seem to really do anything with it."

Rob smiled, "It doesn't really have much functionality until you're on board. On the ship, you'll be able to see the various activities going on, make dinner reservations at one of the specialty restaurants, and check your on-board account.

"But there is one thing that I know is new, since it was only introduced by a few cruise lines a little over a year ago," Rob continued. "A couple of cruise lines teamed up to find a better way to conduct lifeboat drills."

Ben's intrigued look was as sexy as hell. "Really? Tell me more since that always seemed like it took such a long time."

"Yes, it did," Rob agreed. "But it's important, so they worked hard and came up with something called MusterPlus. Basically, you can watch a video on the app and then check a box that says you've watched it and understand what you have to do in an emergency. The video will also be playing on the televisions in all cabins during embarkation. Once you've done that, you head to the muster station indicated on your cruise card and check-in with a safety rep that's stationed there until the ship sets sail. They check you off a list and you're done."

"Wow, sounds great, and so easy. I also got some kind of wristband-thing with the cruise line's logo on it. My assistant sent it to me since I've been traveling, but it was waiting here for me when I arrived. I must confess I really didn't pay much attention to it and didn't read any of the paperwork with it," Ben said, looking a bit embarrassed.

"Ha! No worries," Rob chuckled. "I'm sure you're not the only one. That's your OceanAccess device. There's a metal disc in the wristband. It's removable and the ship sells accessories like a necklace and fancy metal wrist bands that you can use with the disc. It pretty much replaces your cruise card. It will automatically unlock your cabin door when you get near it, and bar servers and gift shop staff have devices that can read the disc so you can use it to make purchases. And it works with the app on your phone; you can even order a drink on your phone and the disc knows where you are on the ship, so someone can deliver the drink to you."

"That's amazing!" Ben exclaimed. "Cruising has come a long way in the past few years."

"It sure has," Rob agreed. He glanced at his watch. "What time do we have to leave for the restaurant?"

Ben checked the time on his phone and said, "We should leave soon." He signaled Carlos and asked him to put the drinks on his room bill.

"I just want to run up to my room and grab a jacket. I forgot to bring it with me when I came down earlier," Rob explained.

"No problem, I'll meet you at the door."

———

THEY WERE both quiet on the taxi ride to the restaurant, but it wasn't uncomfortable. Ben felt like he had known Rob for years instead of just days and he was surprised by how good that felt. He realized that while he had a few close friends and many acquaintances in his life, he hadn't had anyone special for a long time and part of him hoped that Rob could be that special someone.

When they arrived at the restaurant, Ben paid the taxi driver and Rob headed toward the front door. There was a breeze coming off the water and Rob was glad he'd grabbed his jacket before they left. He held the door open for Ben and they walked up to the host standing near a podium just inside.

"*Una reserva para Rockingham,*" Ben said.

"*Sí,* right this way, gentlemen," the host replied, then led them to a table overlooking the water. They sat and, handing them menus, the host said, "*¡Buen provecho!*" and walked away.

Rob hadn't said anything, and Ben was a bit concerned. "Is everything okay, Rob? You seem awfully quiet."

Rob looked at him and, smiling sadly said, "Yeah, I'm just thinking that the last cruise I was on was two and a half years ago with Alan. I had no idea at the time that would be our last cruise together."

Ben's heart hurt for Rob. He reached over and took his hand, "I'm so sorry, Rob. I can't imagine how difficult this must be for you. Did you want to skip dinner and just go back to the hotel?"

Rob looked into Ben's eyes and sighed. "No, absolutely not. I'm just being a bit maudlin. Pay no attention to me. If Alan was here, he'd tell me to snap out of it and enjoy myself. He'd say, *'Damn it, Rob. You're here with a handsome man about to have a great meal so just relax and enjoy yourself. Don't be an idiot'.*" Rob laughed. "And he'd be right. Let's have some wine and enjoy ourselves. And if I'm not mistaken, we still have a lot more cruise chat to get to."

Ben removed his hand. "Okay, wine. Do you want to stick with a Tempranillo, or try something different?"

"I'll let you decide. I'm definitely having seafood so perhaps a white would be better, but honestly, I have no problem drinking red wine with fish."

"White sounds good to me, actually. They have several Albariños on the wine list. I'll choose one of them," Ben offered.

The waiter approached and Ben ordered a bottle of the Albariño. As the waiter left to get the wine, they picked up their menus and thought about food. They decided on *jamón* and grilled shrimp to start and then, after some deliberation, agreed on the *zarzuela de mariscos* for two.

The pace was very leisurely, and as they ate and drank, they talked more about the upcoming cruise.

"What type of cabin do you have on the ship, Ben?"

"I'm in a penthouse suite. My assistant Julie made all the

arrangements for me, but she said that I deserved a suite. She also said that she knew I might end up just hanging around in my cabin all the time, so I should have something large with a nice balcony. She knows me too well."

"Ha," Rob responded. "I think she and Sam would get along really well. She sounds just as controlling as Sam."

"Oh, you have no freakin' idea, Rob." agreed Ben, chuckling.

"I'm in a suite too," Rob admitted. "I'm in one of two Celestial Suites on the ship. They're up on Deck 18, part of the balcony overlooks the pool area."

"Wow! That sounds amazing. Any chance I could get a tour sometime?" Ben asked.

Abso-fucking-lutely! Rob thought, but he said, "Certainly. You're welcome any time.

"I must admit, even though Alan and I have stayed in suites a few times in the past, I've never had a suite quite this large before. When the cruise line announced this class of ship and we first saw the cabin floor plans and then photos, we decided to splurge. I'm really looking forward to seeing it in person.

"Okay," Rob continued, after taking a breath, "But now I've gotten off track, which always happens when I start talking about cruises. What I wanted to say is that there's a special line at the pier for suite passengers. It's usually shorter and we should be able to board the ship faster. You'll drop off your luggage with one of the stevedores that handle getting all the luggage on board, then head into the terminal to check-in. There'll be lots of staff around, just show one of them your boarding pass and they'll direct you to the right line."

"Which reminds me," Ben interrupted. "Do you want to

get a cab together tomorrow? It makes sense as we're both going to the same place."

"That's perfect," Rob agreed. "We can have breakfast and then head to the pier around eleven. Does that sound okay?"

"Yeah, that sounds great." Ben glanced at his watch. "Holy shit, we've been here over two hours! I had no idea."

"Me neither. Good food and great conversation, the time just flew by," said Rob.

He looked around for the waiter and when he saw him, signaled for the check. When the waiter brought it over, Rob handed him his credit card. After the waiter ran it through the portable card reader, he handed the terminal to Rob, who added a tip and signed the screen.

The waiter handed Rob a receipt and his card, saying "*Gracias. Buenas noches, señores.*"

As they exited the restaurant, Ben looked around for a taxi. He was just explaining to Rob that it might be a few minutes before a taxi showed up, when a cab pulled into the restaurant parking area, dropping off a couple of passengers.

Ben asked the driver if he was available and when the driver nodded, they climbed in the back seat. While they rode quietly back to the hotel, Ben was trying to think of how he could tell Rob that he was feeling something for him, without making it sound awkward. Unfortunately, he hadn't come up with anything that sounded right in his head by the time they reached the hotel.

Ben paid the driver. They got out of the taxi and entered the hotel. As they rode the elevator up to their floor, Ben had an idea. When the doors opened, Ben said, "Rob, can I walk you to your room? There's something I'd like to tell you."

"Sure," replied Rob. He used his key card to unlock his

door and they both stepped in. Rob flipped the switch to turn on the light, then turned to Ben and said, "So...what did you want to tell me?"

Ben hesitated for a moment, then looking into Rob's eyes said, "Fuck, I didn't think this would be so difficult."

Rob sighed, "It's okay, I understand, just say it."

Ben said, "Rob, may I kiss you?"

"I...um, what?" Rob looked stunned. His eyes locked with Ben's.

Ben said, "I really want to kiss you."

Rob nodded and their lips met. The kiss was sweet and soft and tender and felt oh, so right.

They parted and Ben said, "Thank you. I've wanted to do that since dinner last night."

"You mean we wasted a whole day when we could have been kissing?" Rob joked. "I've *wanted* you to kiss me since dinner last night."

"Fuck," Ben said. "I don't think the day was wasted, but hell yeah, there could have been more kissing!"

"C'mere," Rob murmured, stepping closer to Ben and claiming his mouth. This time the kiss wasn't soft or tender. It was hot and needy. When Ben's tongue slid along his lips, Rob opened up to him and their tongues battled for dominance.

Rob cradled the back of Ben's head with one hand while the other slid down his back and rested on the top of his ass. Ben grabbed Rob's ass with both hands and pulled him closer, feeling Rob's hard length against his own.

Their lips parted, they both took a breath then went back for more, moaning into each other's mouths. After a few more moments they parted, both breathing heavily.

"Wow." Ben said.

"Yeah. Wow." Rob agreed.

They looked at each other and smiled. "So," Ben started, "I guess I should explain."

"Okay," said Rob, sitting on the edge of the bed and motioning for Ben to take the loveseat.

"For much of my life, I thought I was bisexual," Ben started. "I always found guys and girls attractive and didn't make a big deal of it. I had a boyfriend for a short time when I was in college, but we were both pretty much in the closet at that point. After we broke up, I met Caroline and eventually married her. We started to drift apart a few years after we had Kyle and we both agreed that divorce was probably the best option for us. Neither one of us was ready for marriage. We raised Kyle together as much as we could, and I'm happy to still be friends with her. We're better as friends than we were as a married couple. At one point I told Caroline about the boyfriend I had in college and it was never an issue for her. I also told Kyle I was bi a few years ago. I got the feeling he might also be bisexual, so I told him as a way to let him know that I didn't care who he was attracted to. He was fine with it, and while he hasn't come out to me or anything, it wouldn't surprise me if one day he said he was dating a guy."

Ben paused, grateful for Rob's encouraging silence.

Finally, Ben said, "There was one guy a few years ago. He was an up-and-coming actor and we were both extremely discreet, as he wasn't ready to come out of the closet. We only got together a couple of times, but I will say that he taught me a few things!" He smiled briefly at that memory, but then shook his head, saying, "Ah well, it would never have worked out anyway. He was a lot younger than me, and it was really just a fun fling for the both of us. As I've gotten older, I think I'm actually demisexual. Do you know what that is?"

"Yes," answered Rob. "You need to feel an emotional attachment to someone, right?"

"Exactly," Ben said. "In some ways, I think I'm still working through my feelings about who I am. All I know is, when we met yesterday, I immediately felt some connection and I knew I wanted to spend more time with you."

"I get it," Rob started, once Ben stopped speaking. "Because I also felt something when we met yesterday. And that's never happened to me before. Maybe if we work together, we can figure out if this is really something?"

'Um," Ben teased. "So, you think you might want to go out with me again?" He smiled coyly.

Rob replied, smiling. "Yes, I'd love to go out with you again. But fair warning, I'm gonna need some time. Some days, I can't get outta my own head, but if you can put up with my trying to deal with all of this, then yes, I'd love to try."

Ben looked at him. "It sounds like we both have things that we need to work on and doing it together sounds like a great plan to me."

Ben stood and pulled Rob up from the bed. He kissed him lightly and said, "Okay, I'm going to go to my room now because if I stay here, I'm gonna do something I shouldn't. I'll meet you for breakfast at nine o'clock."

Rob kissed him one more time. "It's a date. Knock on my door at nine."

———

ROB SHUT THE DOOR, sighing.

Wow, I totally misread that, didn't I? I thought for sure Ben was going to tell me that he was getting a weird gay vibe from me and as flattered as he was, he just didn't feel that way toward me. I was convinced I'd have to lock myself in my suite for the week to avoid him.

But he kissed me! And I actually kissed him back. I can't believe I did that.

Rob undressed, slipped under the covers and, with a smile on his face, thought about that kiss.

CHAPTER 5

At exactly nine o'clock, Ben knocked on Rob's door. The door swung open immediately, as if Rob was standing right there, waiting. "Good morning!" Ben leaned in and gave him a quick peck on the lips. "Good morning, Rob. Are you ready?"

"Yeah, let me just grab my phone."

"How did you sleep?" Ben asked, as they headed downstairs.

"Extremely well. I fell asleep with a smile on my face and woke up exactly the same way. I think *you* may have had something to do with that."

"That's funny," Ben grinned. "I went to sleep smiling as well. And I'm pretty sure I was in the same condition when my alarm sounded this morning. You're obviously having a good effect on me."

Getting off the elevator Rob turned to Ben, "Oh, by the way, I called the car service I used to get to the hotel from the airport and requested a car to take us to the cruise terminal. I wanted to make sure we'd have enough room, since we both have luggage. Those taxis we rode in yesterday were tiny. A car will be here at eleven."

"That's a great idea. Thanks."

For breakfast that morning, Rob opted for some whole grain toast with butter and jam, along with his yogurt and fresh fruit. Almost as an afterthought, he also grabbed a couple of slices of bacon. "I didn't see the bacon yesterday," he said.

"I didn't either, so I'll take extra today," Ben agreed with a wink. He proceeded to grab several slices of bacon along with some fruit, a roll, and a spoonful of jam.

"Did you finish packing yet?" Rob asked. "Remember to put anything you might need right away in your carry-on. It may take a few hours before your luggage arrives in your cabin. Also, if you can get to it easily, put on your OceanAccess wristband before we leave. It will help speed up check-in."

"Thanks for the reminder. I'm almost done packing. I just have to add my shaving kit to my suitcase and put my Kindle in my backpack. By the way, would it be okay if we exchanged numbers?" Ben asked as he held up his phone.

"Of course." Rob unlocked his phone and handed it to Ben. Ben did the same and they added in their info. Rob was happy to see that Ben used an iPhone just like he did. Perhaps some FaceTime would be in their future?

A LITTLE WHILE LATER, they had both checked out of their rooms and were sitting in the lobby with the luggage when Rob's phone chimed. He checked the screen, then turned to Ben, "The car's outside."

They walked out of the hotel, happily seeing a Mercedes SUV with plenty of room for them and their luggage.

Fifteen minutes later, they were standing at the terminal, handing over their luggage to a stevedore who then directed them to the building entrance. As they neared the door, they saw a cruise line representative checking passenger boarding passes. They both pulled out their copies and presented them to the rep.

Seeing the 'suite' designation on the passes she said, "Take a left as you enter and look for the signs that say Suite Check In. It's not too busy yet, so you'll most likely be able to board pretty quickly."

There was no line at the suite check-in area, so they were taken care of immediately. After presenting their passports, their OceanAccess bands were scanned, and their photos were taken. Then they were handed a ship's map along with their OceanSail cards.

Walking onto the ship, Ben asked, "Why do I need this card if I have the band?"

"Some folks don't like the band," Rob explained. "They think it means that someone knows where they are every minute and that feels intrusive. There are folks who don't even get the band for that very reason. I, on the other hand, love it. I think technology is great!"

As they reached the entrance to the ship, they took turns

as their wrist bands were scanned and they were welcomed aboard. The security personnel that scanned them in waved over a staff member who approached them and said, "May I show you to your suite?"

"We're actually in two different suites," Rob replied.

"No problem," the staff member replied. She called over a colleague and said, "Ingrid and I can take care of both of you."

The four of them boarded an elevator and one of the staff pressed two floor numbers. When they reached the Caribe Deck, where Ben's cabin was located, he and Ingrid stepped off.

Ben turned to Rob and said, "I'll call you in a little while." Rob nodded as the elevator doors shut.

The other staff member, Marya, said "Is this your first time on the *Ocean Wanderer*, sir?"

"Yes, it is, although I've sailed with Ocean Cruises before. I was on the *Ocean Traveler* a few years ago."

"Welcome back to Ocean Cruises, and welcome aboard the *Wanderer*. I hope you enjoy your time with us."

"Thank you," Rob replied. "I'm sure I will."

They reached the Sky Deck and Rob followed Marya to his cabin door. The screen mounted next to the door welcomed him as he opened the door.

"May I show you where everything is, sir?" Marya asked.

"Thanks," Rob replied, "but I'm sure you have many more passengers to tend to. I'll be okay."

"Very good, sir. If you need anything, just press '3' on your phone for the suite concierge. And again, welcome aboard."

Marya left and Rob shut the door. He dropped his mini-backpack on the sofa and left his wheeled carry-on near the door. He wanted to look around before he did anything. *Oh my goodness. Two bedrooms, two bathrooms, living room, dining room and a huge wraparound balcony! It may have been overkill for just the two of us, but Alan would have loved this!*

Rob stopped, feeling a bit stunned. While that thought made him a little sad, he quickly realized it was more bitter-sweet than sad. He *was* feeling better about all of this, after all. And he smiled as it dawned on him that Ben had a lot to do with that.

At that moment, his phone rang. He pulled it out of his pocket and saw Ben's name on the screen.

"Hi there," he said. "How's your suite?"

"Hi yourself," Ben answered. "The suite is amazing, but I'm sure not as grand as yours."

Rob laughed, "Well maybe I can arrange a tour for you later!"

"Ha! I'm counting on it, Rob. So, what are you going to do now? I'm not ashamed to admit that I'm pretty excited to be on board and I want to look around."

"Tell you what," Rob suggested, "There's a bar on Deck 8 called the Trident Lounge. It's in the middle of the ship, in the area called Seaside Cove. Meet me there in about ten minutes and we can have a drink, then take a little tour."

"Perfect. See you then." Ben rang off.

———

BEN DIDN'T WANT to wait ten minutes. Pacing the living room of his suite with nervous energy, he felt antsy. As he told Rob, he *was* excited to be on board and he wanted to walk around the ship. But it was more than that, he realized. He wanted to see Rob.

Putting his phone in his front pocket, he walked out the door and headed to the bank of elevators down the hall.

When he got off on Deck 8, he looked at the ship's map prominently displayed on the wall and tried to get his bearings. Locating the Trident Lounge, he set off to find it. He walked through a doorway marked Seaside Cove and stopped. His mouth hung open as he looked around in awe.

If he didn't know better, he'd think he was at some resort on land with tropical plants and walkways and balconies on either side looking over the area. Looking up, he realized there was no covering overhead, just the sky several decks up.

Shaking his head, he began walking, passing a sitting area, a few restaurants, and even a waterfall. He saw a sign for the Trident Lounge and realized it had indoor and outdoor seating with a wraparound bar. He headed to the bar and took a seat on the outdoor side.

A bartender, Lukas from Croatia according to his nametag, approached him. In a deep and lightly accented voice he asked, "May I get you a drink, sir?"

"Thank you, but I'm waiting for someone. I'll order when he gets here. Wow, this ship is amazing."

"Your first time, sir?" Lukas asked.

"Yes. I haven't been on a cruise for several years and it was nothing like this. Sitting here, looking around at all of this, it doesn't even feel like a ship," Ben replied.

"Yes, it's pretty fantastic." Another passenger walked up to the bar, and Lukas went to take his order.

Ben continued to look around, marveling at all he was seeing. As he gazed toward the walkway he'd taken from the elevators, he spotted Rob and grinned excitedly.

Rob smiled back and headed over. When he got close

enough, Ben stood up and hugged him. "This is spectacular," he exclaimed. "It doesn't seem like we're on a ship."

"I know," Rob agreed. "It's pretty amazing."

As soon as Rob was seated, Lukas appeared to ask if they wanted drinks.

Rob quickly scanned the bottles behind the bar. "Yes, Ketel One Citroen is my favorite; I'd like that on the rocks, please. With a twist."

"And I'll have Buffalo Trace on the rocks, please," Ben added. He'd noticed the row of bourbon bottles when he first sat at the bar.

"Certainly," Lukas said, as he began to make their drinks.

Placing the glasses on napkins in front of them, he picked up a portable scanner and waved it over each of their Ocean-Access bands. "Thank you, Mr. Robert and Mr. Bentley."

Rob smiled and said, "I love how cruise staff always uses a title with someone's first name. So, Bentley, huh?"

Ben grinned, "Yeah. English mom, remember?"

"Oh, I do. I just hadn't thought of Bentley. I've only ever seen you referred to as 'Ben' and I just figured it was Benjamin," Rob said.

"I wasn't overly fond of 'Bentley' when I was a kid and decided I would only answer to 'Ben.' It's not so bad now, but at this point, no one really uses it. And when my brother's in a teasing mood, it's usually 'Benny' which, for the record, I hate."

Rob looked like he was going to tease him, so Ben quickly added, "But enough about my name." He raised his glass and looking around the ship toasted, "Here's to new adventures!"

"To new adventures!" Rob chimed in. They touched glasses and sipped.

They watched passengers approach the bar to place orders while Lukas and another bartender quickly and efficiently made drinks. "I've been meaning to ask you, Ben, what made you decide to become an actor?"

Ben thought for a moment. "I wasn't really into sports all that much in high school and a couple of my friends were in the drama club. They convinced me to give it a try and I found I was good at it. I stuck with it in college while I was studying business, but I really didn't know what I wanted to do.

"At the end of my senior year, I was approached by a talent scout who saw me in the university's production of *Twelve Angry Men*. He thought I had potential and wanted to know if I planned on pursuing a career in acting. He managed to get me a couple of jobs in commercials and I got noticed. The rest, as they say, is history."

"You've certainly done well. I'd say you made a good choice. Is making a movie as exciting as it seems?"

Rob laughed. "While there have been some exciting times, it's often really tedious. Depending on the director, and how good your co-stars are, you might have to redo a particular scene many times until everyone is satisfied. It can take hours or even days just to get a short scene finished.

"On the other hand, I've had the opportunity to work with stunt people to learn how to fall so that I don't get hurt, and I've learned a few foreign accents and how to shoot a gun. So yeah, some of it is fun and exciting, I guess. I'm proud of most of the movies I've made, but I am getting to the point where I'd like to slow down a bit. As I get older, I'm starting to realize that life is short and I want to enjoy myself a bit more, so I'm more interested in working on a few projects that I really believe in rather than going for things that will be huge block-buster hits."

"I admire you for that," Rob admitted. "Most folks would just go for the money regardless of the project, even if it meant going against their better judgement."

"I couldn't do that and live with myself," Ben confessed. "If a script is garbage—and believe me, I've been offered a lot that are—I refuse to do it no matter how much money they're offering. I won't compromise my beliefs. I have to respect myself and what I choose to do."

"Wow, this got a little heavier than I expected when I first asked the question," Rob said, "but it just proves that you're a good man, Ben."

Ben responded with a tip of his head and a wry smile, "Thanks."

CHAPTER 6

Saturday, October 5 – Later the same day, aboard *Ocean Wanderer*

After they finished their drinks and conversation, Ben and Rob wandered through the rest of Seaside Cove. Rob pointed out the various restaurants, shops, and bars, including a wine bar which also served tapas. They exited at the ship's forward bank of elevators and stairs and walked down three flights to Deck 5.

"This is the Promenade," Rob announced. "Most larger ships have a vertical central atrium that spans three of four decks, but Ocean Cruises decided to go horizontal several years ago and this is the result."

Ben stared in awe at what could only be described as a shopping mall at sea. It was an enormous space three decks high that was the same length as the Seaside Cove area they had just left. There were shops and restaurants down both sides of the wide walkway, including a pizzeria and an English pub. In one corner, Ben spotted a champagne bar, and across from that was a Guest Services Counter. And while there were people everywhere, the space was large enough that it didn't seem overly crowded.

"This is amazing!" he said. "It looks nothing like the ship I was on before."

"Yeah," Rob concurred. "Some lines are really pushing the envelope. They've done some amazing things."

By now they had reached the other end of the promenade and Rob suggested they head up to Deck 16 and check out the pool area.

They got off the elevator and walked around the corner, through sliding glass doors that opened and closed automatically. There was a light breeze, but the sun was shining brightly as they walked past one of the main pools.

Rob pointed to the other side of the ship. "Because the center area is open and looks down into Seaside Cove, there's another pool on the other side."

"I know I've said this before, but wow. Just...wow."

Rob glanced at his watch, "It's been a few hours since breakfast. Are you hungry?" he asked Ben. "There's a grill over there that serves burgers and fries, and there's also a buffet back there." He indicated with his thumb over his shoulder.

"A burger sounds great, actually," Ben replied.

They headed over to the grill and each got a burger and some fries. There was a toppings bar at the end of the grill where they could add condiments to their burgers. Rob got some lettuce and mayo along with some ketchup on the side for his fries. Ben took some sliced tomatoes and pickles, then added some mayonnaise to his plate. Sitting down at a table off to the side, they had a great view of the Barcelona skyline. A bar server approached and asked if they wanted a beverage. They decided on beer and the server left to get their drinks.

A few minutes later, the server returned with their beers and they tucked in. "Oh my God, this is delicious," Rob declared, wiping his mouth. "It's so juicy."

"These fries are crispy and have just the right amount of salt," Ben added, dipping a fry into some mayo. "This is heavenly."

AFTER LUNCH they walked around the deck, Ben becoming a bit more familiar with where things were located on that level. When they reached the aft elevators again, Rob said, "My cabin's not far from here, perhaps you'd like to see it?"

"I think that sounds like a great idea," Ben replied, smiling.

They rode up to Deck 18 and, exiting the elevator, Rob headed around the corner to the right and Ben followed. As the sensors once again 'recognized' him, the screen near his suite door changed to a welcome message and Rob opened the door.

"I have to say, I do find that a little freaky," Ben admitted.

Rob grinned, "Yeah, I get it. The first time I sailed on a ship with OceanAccess, it freaked me out, too. But I got used to it quickly 'cause it's so convenient."

When they walked in, Rob noticed that the cabin attendant had delivered his luggage while he was out.

Ben followed Rob into the suite. His gaze swept the space,

taking in his surroundings. "Wow, this is fantastic!" he exclaimed.

"Let me give you the nickel tour," Rob replied.

"Okay, but can you make it quick? 'Cause there's something I gotta do," Ben said, grinning suspiciously.

Rob paused, a bit confused. "Oh, I'm sorry, Ben. If you need to do something, we can do the tour later. It's fine."

Ben stepped closer to Rob and whispered, "Actually, the only thing I gotta do is this."

He wrapped his arms around Rob and kissed him. Rob placed his hands on either side of Ben's face and returned the kiss. They took their time, enjoying the taste and feel of each other. When the kiss ended, Rob smiled and said, "Forget the nickel for the tour, I like this a lot better."

Without leaving Ben's arms, he jerked his head toward the room. "So, this is the dining area and that's the living room. If you want to see more, I'll need another kiss."

Ben chuckled and kissed him gently. They peered in the doorway to the right and Rob said, "This will be Sam's room when she boards next week."

The room featured a queen bed with a flat screen TV mounted on the wall opposite the bed. The decor was tastefully done in shades of pale green and peach. On the far side of the room, he could see sliders out to the deck. To the right, a small bathroom was visible through an open door.

Rob grabbed Ben's hand and led him back through the living room and dining area then walked through the doorway on the left. The spacious master bedroom was decorated in the same shades of green and peach, but was larger and featured a king bed, built-in desk, and large closet area. The luxurious master bath boasted a whirlpool tub, separate shower, and large marble vanity. The wall above the tub featured a large mosaic seascape.

"Wait until you see the balcony," Rob said excitedly, "it's amazing."

Still holding hands, they walked through the living room to the sliding doors and out to the balcony.

"Holy crap!" Ben exclaimed. "It's huge."

The balcony ran the full width of the suite and overlooked the pool deck. It also wrapped around to the side of the ship, where it would overlook the ocean when the ship was at sea. In addition to a round table with chairs, there were also four lounge chairs and, hidden away on the side of the balcony that overlooked the sea, a hot tub.

"I've never seen anything like this," Ben told Rob, smiling. "And you get to spend three weeks here, huh? Tough life."

Rob laughed. He could tell by the look on Ben's face that he was just giving him a hard time. "Hey," he replied, "someone's gotta do it."

They stood at the balcony railing, watching people mingle near the pool. It was a sunny day, around seventy degrees, and a few passengers were in the pool and several more were sunbathing.

Ben put his arm around Rob, hugging him close. "Is this okay?"

"It is. We've only known each other for a few days, but this feels really comfortable. And for the record, I love hugs."

"Noted."

"Oh, did you want something to drink?" Rob asked, gesturing into the cabin. "I've got a stocked mini-bar. There should be beer, vodka, bourbon, and some sodas."

"A bourbon on the rocks would be great, thanks."

Rob turned to head into the suite and Ben followed. Rob went to the small bar in the dining area, opened the mini-fridge, and pulled out the ice bucket. Filling two glasses with ice, he used the tiny bottles of bourbon and vodka to make drinks for each of them. He turned and saw Ben sitting on the sofa waiting for him.

"This is a really nice room," Ben said, looking around.

The decor was done in shades of off-white and tan with a few accents of chocolate brown and teal, and featured a pair of upholstered chairs along with the sofa and a coffee table. A large screen TV hung on the wall opposite the sofa, and colorful paintings were hung on other walls.

"Yes," Rob agreed. "They did a great job with the decor. It's all very tasteful and well done."

He handed a drink to Ben and sat beside him on the sofa. "Would you like to have dinner with me tonight?" he asked. "I was thinking of going to the Poseidon Steakhouse. It's in Seaside Cove and they have an outdoor seating area which might be nice."

"Poseidon, like the ship that flipped over in those movies? That's a bit morbid, isn't it?" Ben asked, his eyes wide in mock surprise.

"Actually, I think they mean the Greek god of the sea," Rob replied, laughing.

"In that case, I'd love to," Ben said, smiling.

"Is around eight o'clock, okay?" Rob asked.

Ben nodded and sipped his drink.

Rob reached for the phone on the end table and pressed '3' for the suite concierge.

"Would it be possible to get a reservation at the Poseidon Steakhouse tonight? Something around eight, if you have it," he said when someone answered. "No, it will be for two of us. Mr. Rockingham in cabin...I'm sorry, hold on a moment please.

"What's your cabin number, Ben?"

"10234."

"Mr. Rockingham in suite 10234," Rob continued. He sipped his drink while he waited and then said, "Yes, eight thirty will be fine. Thank you."

As he hung up the phone, he turned to Ben and said, "We're all set."

At that moment, a voice came over the ship's intercom informing the passengers that the ship would be departing in a few minutes.

"Do you want to stand out on the balcony and watch as the ship leaves Barcelona?"

"Sure."

They rose and walked out onto the balcony, picking a spot near the corner so they could see the skyline as well as the groups of people near the pool. Bar staff were walking through the crowds with trays of drinks, and music was playing over the loudspeakers as the sail-a-way party began.

Ben raised his glass toward the city and said, "See you in a week!"

They swayed gently to the music and sipped their drinks as the party continued on the Pool Deck below. Occasionally, people would gaze up at them and they raised their drinks, caught up in the party atmosphere. Eventually, folks drifted away, and the two men went back inside.

"I should head back to my cabin," Ben said. "Hopefully my luggage has arrived and I can unpack. I don't want to nap at this point, but I think I'll feel more refreshed if I take a shower and change before dinner."

"I was thinking the same thing," Rob admitted. "Why don't I come to your cabin around eight and we can head to dinner from there?"

"Sounds good," Ben leaned into Rob and kissed him. "I'll see you later."

After Ben left, Rob rolled his suitcase and carry-on into the bedroom. Laying them on the bed, he unzipped the large bag and started to put things away. As he hung things up in the closet, he picked out a shirt for later and hung it in the bathroom, hoping the steam from his shower would help relax the few wrinkles he saw.

Once he had unpacked everything from both bags, he tucked them away under the bed and decided to read for a little while before getting ready for dinner. Grabbing his Kindle from the nightstand, he went into the living room and sat on the couch.

JUST BEFORE EIGHT O'CLOCK, Ben was rushing around his cabin, trying to finish dressing. He gazed at the clock on the night-stand. *Shit, he'll be here any minute!*

He went into the bathroom and swiped deodorant under each arm then spritzed a bit of cologne on his chest and quickly combed his hair. Walking back to the bed, he picked up the light-green dress shirt and as he put it on, he heard the doorbell ring.

Sighing, he walked to the door and opened it. Rob stood there looking stunning in a blue oxford shirt and navy slacks.

"Sorry," Ben said. "I'm running just a few minutes behind schedule."

"No worries, we have plenty of time." Rob leaned in for a quick kiss and Ben inhaled, catching a heady scent of cedar and citrus. Ben went back for a second kiss, "Hmmm, you smell good."

Rob grinned, "Thanks, you're not so bad yourself. Is that orange-spice I smell? It's wonderful."

"Yes, and a hint of sandalwood, too. I'm glad you like it. I know I said I wasn't going to nap, but I started reading and fell asleep," Ben said sheepishly. He finished buttoning his shirt and tucked it into his pants. "Let me put on my shoes and I'll be ready."

"Take your time, Ben. It's just eight now. It will only take us a few minutes to walk to the restaurant."

Rob sat on the sofa and looked around. The carpet was a mottled pattern in various shades of gray and blue, nicely complementing the dark teal sofa and matching chairs. Accent pillows in different patterns incorporated the colors, and a bit of pale yellow completed the effect. Understated but comforting. Through an archway, he noticed the king sized bed covered in a dove grey duvet, and more accent pillows gracing the chaise in the corner. The decor was quite different from his own suite, but it was still beautiful.

"I love this suite, Ben. I would definitely consider something like this the next time I sail. The Celestial Suite is a bit over-the-top and definitely too much for one or two people. But when Alan saw the photos in a brochure, he decided we had to book it."

"Yeah, this is spacious, but still has a cozy feel to it," Ben agreed. Putting his OceanAccess wrist band on and grabbing his phone he said, "Okay, I'm ready."

They decided to take the stairs rather than the elevator, as it was only two decks down. Once on Deck 8 they passed through the doors to Seaside Cove and meandered along, taking in the sights. Some passengers were strolling on the walkways, while others sat on benches along the way. As they passed the Trident Lounge, they saw Lukas behind the bar and when he noticed them, he waved.

They waved back and continued on to the Poseidon Steakhouse. Although a few minutes early, Rob checked in with the maitre d'.

They were seated at a table for two in the outdoor area. "It feels like we're in an outdoor café," Ben commented. A white wrought iron railing separated the dining area from the walkway and twinkling lights were woven through it. The tables were set with pristine white tablecloths and a centerpiece of an antique bronze lantern glowed, causing the crystal glasses to sparkle.

A waiter approached and took their drink order, then left them to decide on dinner. For appetizers, Rob selected the French onion soup while Ben opted for the shrimp cocktail. They both decided on filet mignon for their entrée, and they chose to share scalloped potatoes and creamed spinach to accompany the main course.

They sipped their drinks and Ben asked, "Do you have any specific plans for this cruise? Any place you're thinking of visiting while we're in port?"

"Not really. I planned on just taking it easy most days, although I did see a shore excursion that looked interesting when we're in Civitavecchia. A lot of passengers will opt for

Rome, but I've been there a few times before. There's a trip to an area called Tuscania that sounded interesting. After a short visit in the town, you head to a farm where they grow olives and grapes among other things. Then lunch with ingredients grown right at the farm. It sounded more interesting than either Rome or staying on the ship."

"That does sound great. That's in a couple of days, right?"

"Yes, we're at sea tomorrow then Genoa the next day. Civitavecchia is the day after that. I haven't booked the trip yet. Would you be interested in joining me if there's still room? We could stop by the Shore Excursion Desk later and see."

"I'd like that. I hadn't planned on doing anything at all except relax this trip but visiting Tuscania sounds like a lot of fun. Thanks for inviting me. You're certainly a wealth of information; it's like having my own travel specialist."

They enjoyed a leisurely dinner, chatting about different places they had been and what they liked or didn't like about certain cities. They were going to skip dessert, but then Ben suggested perhaps they could share something, and Rob caved faster than he intended. "I'm going to need to find the gym at some point if I keep eating like this!"

Ben laughed. "You look fine to me. But we can both look for the gym if it will make you feel better."

When the last forkful of pie had been consumed, Rob sighed, "The lemon meringue pie was delicious, but I'm still glad we shared. I need to pace myself since I'm on this ship for three weeks."

After dinner, they walked to the Shore Excursion Desk on Deck 5 to inquire about the Tuscania trip. There was still space, so they booked it. Martina, who took care of them, explained that the tickets would be delivered to their cabins within the next day or so. She also reminded them that they should arrive together at the meeting place on the morning of the excursion to ensure that they would be on the same bus for the trip.

"Would you like to join me for a nightcap?" Ben asked.

"Sure. The Coral Reef Bar is down there," Rob pointed, indicating the other end of the Promenade. "Alan and I used to make a game of having at least one drink in every bar on a ship when we first started cruising. As the ships got larger with more and more bars, it became quite a challenge." His eyes widened a bit and he shook his head, laughing.

"Well as long as you didn't try to do that in a single day, I don't see anything wrong with it."

"Oh, remind me to tell you about the time Sam and I tried something like that. It wasn't pretty."

Ben laughed heartily, then sobered. "I feel so comfortable with you, Rob. Thank you for sharing your time and all your cruise knowledge. This trip is so much better with you than it would have been by myself."

"Happy to help," Rob said, "I'm enjoying the time spent with you, too."

The bar was surprisingly empty, so they grabbed a table and chairs off to one side and each ordered bourbon on the rocks when a server appeared. They sat in companionable silence and enjoyed the soft piped in music. "I'm amazed that it's not more crowded. After all, there are thousands of people on board," Ben commented.

"I think it has more to do with the fact that it's the first night of the cruise. Some folks don't plan to arrive ahead of time and those from the States were flying all night and are probably exhausted."

After they finished their drinks, they took the elevator up to the Caribe Deck and Rob walked Ben to his cabin. "I'm just getting extra steps in," he said, chuckling. "Perhaps I can put off looking for the gym for another day or two."

When they arrived at Ben's door, he turned to Rob, "Thank you for a lovely evening." He leaned toward Rob and kissed him. "Would you like to meet for breakfast in the morning?"

"That would be nice. Call me, but not before nine please, I'm hoping to sleep in a bit tomorrow. And I had a wonderful time tonight, too." Rob looked at Ben then leaned in and they kissed one more time.

CHAPTER 7

Rob opened his eyes and looked at the clock on the nightstand. Six forty-three. Damn! He'd been tossing and turning for a while but couldn't fall back to sleep. Sighing, he got up and padded into the bathroom.

He relieved himself, then washed his hands and splashed water on his face. If he wasn't going to sleep any more, he needed coffee. At the bar in the dining area, he followed the instructions on the small coffee maker, then listened as the coffee slowly dripped into the cup. While he waited, he checked his emails but there was nothing of importance and he had no new texts.

When the coffee maker finished, he lifted the cup and inhaled deeply, enjoying the rich aroma. He took a sip and sighed. He always enjoyed that first sip.

Planning to read a bit, he retrieved his Kindle from the nightstand, but then noticed his travel journal. He'd left it on the desk in the bedroom when he unpacked yesterday.

Rob had started keeping a journal of his and Alan's trips many years ago and, after a couple of false starts, decided on a Circa notebook. It consisted of plastic discs for the binding with specially punched paper so he could easily add, remove, and rearrange pages as needed.

He was usually much better at writing a journal entry every day, but he'd felt so off-kilter when he finally decided to go forward with this trip that he'd never even taken the journal out of his suitcase when he got to the hotel in Barcelona.

"Well," he said aloud, "You've got time now, so start writing." He picked up the journal and sat down at the dining table.

He opened the book and turned to the table of contents. Taking the pen from the elastic loop on the back cover, he added a new line: Ocean Wanderer - Spain And Transatlantic Crossing – October 2019.

He flipped the pages and saw that the last page in the trip section was the final entry from his last cruise with Alan over two years ago.

He reread the entry and smiled sadly, thinking of the fun they'd had on that trip. *Okay, stop reliving the past and get on with it.*

He turned to the last section of the journal, where he kept extra blank pages. There was writing on the first page in this section, but the penmanship was not his own. The neat, cursive scroll was familiar though.

As he began reading, his breath caught in his throat and his eyes welled with tears, spilling onto the page.

Oh Alan. My Alan!

Rob –

"Here's to all the places we went. And here's to all the places we'll go. And here's to me, whispering again and again and again and again: I love you." – John Green

Hoping this message catches you by surprise as we begin our next trip together. I love how you faithfully write an entry for each day of a trip, but as far as I know, you never look at them again. Just one of the many things I love about you, Robbie.

Where will we go next? The sky's the limit, I guess. All I know is that I want to travel the world with you.

To new adventures!

All my love,

A–

"Will you give me yourself? Will you come travel with me? Shall we stick by each other as long as we live?" – Walt Whitman

THE TEARS WOULDN'T STOP. He pushed the journal aside, not wanting to get any more tears on the page for fear of making the ink run.

He sobbed like he hadn't in a long time. *Oh Alan! Why did you have to die? I wasn't ready for you to leave me! I still love you so much!*

Why was he even on this cruise? Sam convinced him it was a good idea, but now, seeing this message from Alan, he wasn't so sure. He should be home, mourning the loss of his husband. Not enjoying himself on a vacation and meeting a hot guy.

Ben! Oh my God, what was he doing with Ben? It was too soon. He shouldn't be enjoying himself like this!

He grabbed his phone and quickly texted Ben.

> Ben, I'm sorry but I can't meet you for breakfast today. I'm so sorry.

Hopefully Ben wouldn't want to talk or ask why he canceled. He just couldn't deal with all these emotions he was feeling right now. Couldn't deal with trying to explain it all to Ben when he was still trying to figure it all out himself.

His heart ached. He thought of Alan and all the good times they had traveling together, and the tears started flowing all over again.

BEN HEARD his phone buzz and he picked it up from the nightstand. It was seven forty-five and he still had some time before he needed to get up and prepare for the day.

He read Rob's message and was confused. What had happened between last night and this morning? Was Rob ill or something?

> Rob, what's wrong? Are you ill? What can I
> do to help?

He waited a moment but there was no response.

Then he got scared. He thought back to dinner the night before and the time they spent together afterward. Did he do something wrong? Did he say something that offended Rob in some way?

No, everything seemed fine. At Ben's door they had kissed good night and agreed on breakfast today. Nothing seemed amiss.

Was Rob having second thoughts about seeing him? When they talked back at the hotel in Barcelona, they'd agreed that they both had some things to work through, but he had thought that if they tried together it would be okay.

Maybe he should have attempted to talk to Rob a bit more about where things stood between them. They admitted they were attracted to each other, and wanted to see more of each other, but perhaps they should have talked in more detail about what that really meant. Was he moving too fast? Was Rob getting cold feet now? What was going on in his head?

He checked his phone again, but there was still nothing from Rob.

> I'm here if you need me.

He felt helpless. If Rob was dealing with something, he wanted to be there to help. But he figured the best thing to do was wait. Wait and hope that Rob would figure out that he could lean on Ben if he needed to. Giving Rob some space felt like the right thing to do, even though he wanted to run up to his suite and hold him.

Ben showered and dressed in jeans and a navy long-sleeved T-shirt. He decided to try the Cove Café for breakfast. They had passed it in Seaside Cove the day before and Rob had explained that they served a light breakfast and lunch.

He got a toasted bagel with cream cheese, some fresh fruit, and a cup of coffee. He picked a table outside so he could enjoy the view and people-watch. And secretly he hoped that if Rob happened to walk by, they could talk. He wanted so badly to tell Rob that he was here to support him.

But Rob never appeared. Ben tried not to worry too much and once he'd finished his breakfast, he set off on a walk, hoping to burn off some nervous energy.

Ben eventually made his way up to the Pool Deck and looked up at the balcony of Rob's suite. The sheer drapes in front of the sliders were all closed and there didn't seem to be any lights on, so he couldn't see anything except the empty balcony.

He texted Rob one more time.

> I'm worried about you, but I'll leave you alone if you just tell me that you're ok.

He waited a moment and when no message appeared, he sighed and put his phone away.

He'll call or text when he's ready. I need to do something to take my mind off this for now.

It was a bit chilly out on deck, so he headed inside in search of a quiet place to sit.

He studied the ship map near the elevators and saw the Lighthouse Lounge on Deck 19, aft. There, he found a nice quiet space with an almost three-hundred-and-sixty-degree view of the ocean. Consulting the ship's app on his phone, he saw that the bar didn't open until four o'clock, so that explained why it was almost empty.

He chose a chair near the windows overlooking the back of the ship and watched the wake as they moved through the water. He pulled his Kindle out of his back pocket and began to read.

He was totally engrossed in his book when his phone buzzed. He looked at the screen and realized that a couple of hours had passed. He saw a text from Rob stating he was okay but needed more time. Ben felt a huge rush of relief.

Ben stared out at the water. He could get through this. He and Rob really needed to talk. Back in Barcelona when they first kissed and Ben admitted that he might be demi, they agreed they wanted to work together to see if there really was something between them. Rob admitted that he sometimes couldn't get out of his own head, and Ben was afraid that was exactly what had happened to Rob that morning.

I have to be patient and give him some space. But if he'll talk to me, we'll be okay.

Rob heard his phone ding and saw two messages from Ben, but he couldn't think about him right now. He felt too raw. And alone.

What is happening to me right now?

He felt so restless. He walked onto the balcony but as they were out to sea, it felt just a bit too breezy to stay out there.

Back in the suite, he flung himself on the bed and curled up. He tossed and turned a bit, but eventually he slept.

His eyes slowly opened and at first, Rob was confused. Was that all a dream? He looked at the bedside clock and saw that it was almost two in the afternoon. Despite all that sleep, he felt groggy and out of sorts.

He got up and walked into the dining area. Seeing his journal lying open on the table and his now-cold cup of coffee, he knew it was all real.

When his stomach growled, he realized he'd missed both breakfast and lunch. He didn't feel hungry but knew he should eat something. He found a protein bar in his mini-backpack and ate that while he made a new cup of coffee.

You really need to snap out of this, Rob!

But he couldn't. He felt torn and unsure. Mulling it all over, he had an idea.

Opening the message app on his phone, he saw a new text that Ben had sent a few hours earlier.

> I'm worried about you, but I'll leave you
> alone if you just tell me that you're ok.

He quickly replied.

> I'm ok. I need some time. I'm sorry.

He was almost afraid that Ben might respond right away, so he quickly switched to Sam's account, typed a question, then hit Send.

> Are you awake? I really need you.

He stared at the screen, saw three dots and then her response.

Skyping now.

God, he loved her. She was always there for him.

His phone rang and he pressed Accept on the screen. He saw Sam, looking very worried.

"What's wrong, Sweetie?"

"Oh Sam, I'm so confused. You need to help me figure this out."

"Of course. If you don't mind my saying, you look like hell and I can tell you've been crying. And sure, I'll help you. What's going on?"

Rob chuckled. Leave it to Sam to tell him he looked awful but then immediately shift gears and offer assistance.

"Okay, but I need to give you all the background so get comfortable. And you might want to get a beverage. This may take a while."

"Already there, my friend." Sam lifted a large cup into view. "I'm snuggled in bed with coffee. Now tell me what happened."

Rob told her everything that had happened since their last conversation. He didn't leave anything out, including the fact that he had feelings for Ben. And apparently Ben also had feelings for him.

When he got to the part about finding Alan's note in the travel journal earlier that morning, Sam sighed. He walked over to the journal and read the note to Sam, his voice breaking several times and more tears running down his face.

"Oh sweetie, I'm so sorry. I can't imagine what you're feeling."

"It hurts so much, Sam! I think I went a little crazy this morning. But now I'm so confused about my feelings," Rob admitted, wiping his eyes.

"Okay, tell me what you did."

Rob continued his story, explaining how he put off Ben for breakfast and then spent the rest of the morning crying, doubting himself, and sleeping. He confessed that he felt guilty for feeling something for Ben because he still loved Alan, and how that left his heart in knots.

"I should have stayed home. I don't deserve someone else. I should still be mourning Alan."

Sam looked intently at Rob and frowned. "Honey, I love you, but don't be stupid. Listen to yourself; you don't deserve someone else? What kind of shit-talk is that? Of course you deserve to be happy. We all do. If Alan were here, he'd be the first one to tell you that you're being an idiot. You know I'm right."

Rob smiled, "How do you do that? You're saying the things that have been spinning around in my head all day, but when you say it, it sounds reasonable. When I think it, it sounds selfish and wrong."

"It sounds reasonable, because you know I'm right and I would only tell you the truth."

Rob smiled again and even laughed a bit. "Fair enough. I love you, you know. I can't even think of what my life would be without you in it."

"I love you too, silly. Even if you act like an idiot every now and then and let your mind take you to all the wrong places.

And it goes both ways, Rob. I can't imagine my life without you, either."

They chatted a bit more and Rob felt his chest relax and his breathing ease. Yes, he still loved Alan and he missed him terribly, but Sam was right, that didn't mean he didn't deserve happiness, that he didn't deserve someone else.

"So, what do I do now, Sam? I mean, I blew him off this morning. And not in a good way."

Sam snorted. "Behave!" There was a smile in her voice. "First, take a shower and shave, 'cause really Rob, you still look awful. Then get dressed. You'll feel better. Next, call Ben and apologize like hell, but be honest. Tell him you want to see him and when he agrees, go see him and explain what happened this morning. And tell him how it fucked with your head and you kinda went over the edge for a bit."

"You're right. That's exactly what I need to do. But what if he doesn't want to see me?"

"Of course I'm right. You've met me, remember?" Sam giggled. "And yes, he'll agree to see you. Based on what you've told me about the time you two have spent together, it sounds like he's very interested in you and I can tell that you're crazy about him already." She looked at him and smirked. "Trust me."

"I do. And thank you for being there for me, Sam. I owe you. Again."

He thought back to how she had been there when Alan died. She'd spent two weeks in his guest room, taking care of him when he was so lost and helpless.

Sam grinned, "Damn right you owe me! But don't worry, you'll buy me lots of drinks and meals on the ship. Lots and lots of drinks."

Rob laughed, and felt a lightness in his chest. He realized he was feeling so much better and, so long as Ben gave him time to explain, things would be okay.

"I love you Sam. I'll see you in about six days."

"I love you too, Robbie." She hardly ever called him Robbie, but she knew it would make him feel loved. "Remember, I'm here for you any time of the day or night. Call me again if you need to."

"I think it's gonna be okay, but thanks. I'll see you soon."

CHAPTER 8

Sunday, October 6 - *Ocean Wanderer* **at sea, later that day**

Ben paced. He was trying to be patient, but it was difficult. He had returned to his suite hoping that he would hear something more from Rob, but so far, nothing. He had skipped lunch and should probably think about getting something to eat, but his stomach was churning a bit and he wasn't sure he could keep anything down.

What if Rob decided that he wanted nothing more to do with him? Would Ben be able to convince him that there was something real between them? *Was* there something there, or was it just wishful thinking on Ben's part?

No, there was some spark between them. They'd both admitted to feeling it. Hell, Ben *still* felt it. He wanted Rob. Wanted to spend time with him, to get to know him better. Wanted to kiss him, to do more than just kiss him.

What would it feel like to hold Rob's naked body close to his? To feel their hard cocks rub against each other? To plant kisses down his torso and take his time tasting every inch of him?

Argh! His rambling thoughts were getting him nowhere. Well, it was getting him worked up, but that wasn't helping anything right now, was it?

Please, Rob. Please tell me you still want me. Please tell me you want to try.

<hr>

ROB CLOSED the journal and carefully set it on the desk in the bedroom. He paced in the cabin, moving from the bedroom to the living room and back again. This wasn't helping. Why couldn't he settle down? Skyping with Sam had helped a lot. It always did. She could talk him off the ledge like no one else. Well, except Alan. But Alan wasn't here, so he couldn't think about that. He still felt a bit antsy, so he lay down on the bed, trying to calm himself down a bit before he called Ben. He wanted a clear head when they talked. He grabbed his phone, opened his favorite meditation app and picked a ten-minute session that he hoped would calm and center him.

"Okay, Rob," he whispered aloud. "Calm down. Take a deep, cleansing breath." After a few moments, his breathing slowed and he felt himself begin to relax.

"Hey, Robbie. How are you feeling?"

"Alan? What the fuck?! How is this possible? How are you here?" Ben turned and saw Alan lying beside him, smiling.

"You're dreaming, silly. All that worrying and overthinking about Ben really did a number on you. When you started up that meditation app, you drifted off and I decided to pay you a visit.

Man, when you get stuck inside your brain, you really get stuck, dontcha? Stop overthinking it, Rob. Listen to Sam. Ben's a good guy. I like him. And I think he's just what you need. He's calm and doesn't get flustered very easily. He can keep you out of your own head. Probably even better than I could." Alan grinned gently.

"But I miss you so much, Alan. Why did you have to die?"

"Sorry darling, not my fault. The ticker gave out. But enough about me, I'm gone and we can't change that. But you can move on and sweetheart, I think it's time. You need someone else in your life. Take what Ben has to offer. I'm glad he'll be there to keep an eye on you."

"Really, you're not upset?"

"Why would I be upset? He's already fallen really hard for you, Rob. Don't be afraid. I love you."

"I love you too, Alan. Always."

Rob opened his eyes, momentarily disoriented. He looked at his phone and realized that almost forty minutes had passed. Wow. Had Alan really visited his dreams? Somehow, his heart felt lighter than it had before.

Hauling himself off the bed, Rob stripped, and turned on the shower. Once the water had warmed up, he stepped in and washed his hair, then scrubbed at his body, feeling better with each passing minute. He thought back to Alan in that dream–it was a dream, right? It's not like Alan was actually lying next to him in bed, after all. In that moment Rob realized that he could think about Alan and be sad that he was gone, but it wasn't debilitating like it had been before.

Then he remembered Alan's note and the line 'To new adventures!' that he wrote at the end. That was the same thing Ben said when he toasted yesterday at the bar. Yes, this was going to be a new adventure for him. For both of them if they could manage it. Damn it, he did deserve some happiness, right?

He dried off, shaved and combed his hair, before pulling on a pair of jeans and a soft gray Henley.

He was going to call Ben, just as Sam had suggested, but then chickened out at the last minute. Instead, he texted.

Is it OK if I call you?

Almost immediately, his phone rang. It was Ben.

He hit Accept. "Hi."

"Hi, Rob. How are you? I've been worried about you." Rob could hear concern, and a bit of nervousness, in Ben's voice.

"I know and I'm so sorry I made you worry. I had a little meltdown then a long Skype call with Sam; she talked me off the ledge and maybe kicked my ass a little."

"Remind me to send her flowers, okay?" Ben sighed a bit, sounding relieved.

Rob chuckled. "Sure, but we can't spoil her like that all the time. She enjoys it too much."

"So, what's going on, Rob? Are you really okay?" Rob could hear a bit of apprehension creeping back into Ben's voice.

"Yeah, I am." Rob said. Trying to sound convincing so as to ease Ben's worry. "I'm a lot better now, but I'm still a work in progress. I was wondering if we could talk. I'm sorry I shut you out this morning. That wasn't fair to you and I apologize. I just couldn't think straight and needed some time. But how I handled it wasn't fair to you."

He paused, thinking of what to say next.

"So, can we talk? Now, if you have time and if you're willing. I can come down to your suite. Well, if you're in your suite. I just realized I don't even know where you are right now."

"Yes, I'm in my suite and yes, we can talk right now. And you can come here, or I can go to you if that's easier."

"I'd rather come to you, I need to get out of this room for a bit, if that's okay?"

"Sure, come on down. I'll be waiting for you."

After putting on his sneakers, Rob grabbed his phone and headed for the door. Suddenly, he realized he'd forgotten his OceanAccess band and while retrieving it, he tucked his journal under his arm. Ben deserved to see what caused his meltdown.

Rob slowly walked down the corridor to Ben's suite. He felt nervous and anxious and tried to calm his breathing as he walked.

He reached the door and rang the bell.

"Hey, Rob. Please come in."

Rob watched Ben take a step forward then stop, as if he wasn't sure what to do or how to act right now. Rob cringed inwardly, realizing he was the cause of Ben's uncertainty right now.

Rob reached forward and put his arms around Ben, hugging him tight. "I'm so sorry for what I put you through this morning."

"I forgive you, Rob. I just want you to be okay."

They sat, Rob on the sofa and Ben taking one of the chairs as if wanting to give Rob some space.

"Do you want something to drink?"

"Water would be great. I might need something stronger later, though." Rob winked and he saw Ben visibly relax.

Ben got two bottles of water from the fridge and, handing one to Rob, sat back down.

"So even though I wanted to sleep in this morning, I ended up waking up really early. I couldn't fall back to sleep, so I got up and made some coffee. I was going to read for a while, but I saw my travel journal and decided to add a new entry. I'm usually good about adding something new every day I'm on a trip, but I never opened it in Barcelona, so I wanted to catch up."

He smiled at Ben, "I'm blaming you for my lax behavior in keeping up with my entries. You definitely distracted me."

"Sorry, not sorry." Ben grinned back.

"So, I sat at the dining-room table with my coffee and this journal." He turned the book toward Bren, showing him the cover. "This is a photo of Santorini, Greece. I took the photo years ago on the first Mediterranean cruise Alan and I went on. I manipulated the image to give it an artsy look and thought it would make a cool cover. I even designed the inside pages to include the info that I want to remember whenever I travel. It's very special to me; I've been using it for quite a few years.

"I opened it and saw that the last page in the *trips* section was from our last cruise, so I flipped to the back of the book where I keep a section with blank pages. I can add them in when I need to for a new trip."

Rob flipped open the book, showing Ben how it was arranged.

"And when I got to the back section, this is what I found." He took the page containing Alan's note and gently pulled it from the binding disks. He was careful not to tear it so that he could put it back in the journal later.

He handed the page to Ben.

Ben took the page and Rob waited anxiously while he read it. When Ben suddenly looked up, his eyes wide, mouth gaping open, Rob was a little worried.

A tear rolled down Ben's cheek. He stared at Rob, "Oh my God. I'm so very sorry."

Tears filled Rob's eyes again. "Thank you. It was awful. I was in shock. I just sat there and sobbed."

Rob shook his head and looked down, ashamed to meet Ben's gaze. "And then I panicked. I felt guilty for feeling something for you. I felt guilty for not staying home and mourning my dead husband. I couldn't think. So I texted you and said I couldn't meet you for breakfast. I didn't know how to tell you I was having a meltdown, so I just avoided you."

"It's okay. I forgave you, remember? I was just afraid you were sick or something and I felt helpless."

"I *was* sick. Well, heartsick and not thinking clearly. And when I began doubting myself, I just turned inward and probably made it worse."

"Did you stay in your suite the whole time?" Ben asked. When Rob nodded, Ben continued. "I may have taken a walk up on the Pool Deck and tried to look up into your suite, but all I could see was the empty balcony."

"Yeah, I curled up in bed and eventually fell asleep again. When I woke up, I realized that I really needed to talk to Sam. If you haven't figured it out already, she's my go-to shoulder to cry on. She's also the foot that will happily kick my ass when I need it."

Ben laughed. "Well, if I couldn't be there for you..." he started, "...and I totally get why you felt that you couldn't talk to me at that point, so it's okay," he quickly added. "I'm glad you have her in your life. And again, I really need to send her flowers."

"Me too. As soon as I texted her and said I needed her, she Skyped me. It really helped that we could talk face-to-face. She listened while I told her about us hanging out together over the past couple of days and then how I lost it this morning."

Rob smiled, feeling the knot is his stomach untwist. "Then she told me what I needed to hear. She told me that I deserved some happiness even if I didn't think so. And she said that Alan would tell me the same thing if he were here.

"Even though I had thought some of those same things, along with the self-doubt and other thoughts that maybe I didn't really deserve you, when she said it, it resonated in here." He placed his hand over his heart.

"Then she pretty much kicked my ass and told me to clean myself up because I looked like hell," Rob laughed. "And she wasn't wrong. She told me to call you and apologize. She also said that you and I needed to talk more. She's right about that, too. Hell, she's always right, but don't tell her I said that. She thinks it enough for all of us!"

Ben snickered, "My lips are sealed."

"After I spoke with her, I planned to call you, but I was feeling restless, so I used a meditation app to try and calm myself down and I dozed off for a little while. I dreamed about Alan, but it felt like more than a dream. He was lying beside me and told me to listen to Sam and get out of my own head. He also told me to give you a chance. That you would be a good person to have in my life."

Rob paused a moment, figuring out what to say next. "So,

are we okay, Ben? If I try harder to not shut you out, will you give me another chance?”

“Yes, Rob. Like I said before, I understand why you couldn’t talk to me earlier. And yeah, we both need to do a better job about sharing what’s rattling around in our brains. When I admitted to you that I thought I might be demi, we never really spoke much about that. I’m still processing it myself, but I do want us to talk about it.”

Rob nodded. "That sounds great."

“Maybe not today though. I think maybe we’ve talked enough for today,” he grinned at Rob. Then, changing the subject he asked, “Have you eaten?”

“Um, I had a protein bar a few hours ago. I really wasn’t hungry, but I think I could eat now,” Rob answered. “What about you?”

“I had breakfast at the Cove Café and this bottle of water. Yeah, I could eat too.”

“Can we stay in, though? I feel like I ran a marathon or something—I’m exhausted, but relieved, and really don’t feel up to dealing with other people tonight.”

“Yeah, a quiet night sounds good. I know I saw a room-service menu somewhere. Let’s see what’s available.”

“It’s probably in the folder near the phone. The one over on the bar?”

Ben got up and found the folder. He sat next to Rob on the sofa so they could look at it together. Rob nudged closer and put his arm around Ben’s shoulder as they read.

“Hmmm, a Caesar salad and the fettuccine Alfredo with grilled chicken. I need comfort food tonight. And red wine. I think red wine is in order,” Rob said after he had perused the menu.

"That sounds perfect. I think I'll have the same," Ben agreed. "They have a Malbec on the wine list. Is that okay?"

Rob nodded and Ben dialed room service. He placed the order, asking for two bottles of wine.

"Are you trying to get me drunk so you can have your way with me, kind sir?" Rob asked, a twinkle in his eye. "What kind of a boy do you think I am?" he added dramatically.

Ben laughed and turned to face Rob. "No, but I figured we've both had a tough day today. Granted yours was much worse than mine, but still. Neither one of us is driving, and it's just a short elevator ride to your suite, so if we have a bit too much, no harm. We've earned it."

"And if we don't finish the wine today, there's always tomorrow."

CHAPTER 9

Ben rolled over and opened his eyes. The bedside clock read eight-twelve. He felt warmth behind him, it took a moment for him to remember that Rob was there.

Dinner had been nice. Just casual and relaxed while they chatted about a lot of different things: movies, TV shows, books. It had been sweet and comfortable.

And they drank wine. Lots of wine. When the first bottle was empty, Ben opened the second and they'd ended up drinking most of that. At one point, Ben played some music on his phone and they had danced around the living room a bit.

And they kissed.

Then they'd kissed some more. But it hadn't gone any further than that. Well, okay, they *had* made out for a while and they'd both gotten hard, but they stopped before things got out of hand. It had been a very emotional day for Rob; Ben hadn't wanted to overstep.

When Rob had gotten up to leave, he'd been a bit unsteady on his feet. Ben was about to offer to walk him back to his suite when Rob asked if he could stay. He'd explained that he wasn't looking for anything other than maybe a cuddle. He just didn't think he could be alone.

Ben had readily agreed, wanting nothing more than to make Rob feel cared for.

They had taken turns in the bathroom, with Rob using his finger to brush his teeth. Then they undressed, being sure to keep their underwear on, and slid under the covers.

They hugged, then Rob had turned over and offered himself as the little spoon. They fell asleep quickly.

Rob turned to look at the back of Ben's head. "Are you awake?" he whispered.

"Yeah," Ben replied sleepily. "How are you feeling this morning?"

"Great. I slept so well. Thanks for letting me stay. I feel much better this morning."

Ben twisted to face him, "I'm glad. Do you want breakfast? We could order more room service."

"I do want breakfast and lots of coffee. But how about we go somewhere? I'll go back to my cabin so I can shower and change and then we can grab a bite somewhere."

"Okay," Ben leaned forward and kissed him. "I'll pick you up at your place in thirty minutes. Is that good?"

"Sure." Rob got up and reached for his jeans on the chair next to the bed. Ben couldn't help but admire the way his ass filled out his tight, black boxer briefs. Rob pulled his Henley over his head and sat down, slipping on his socks and sneakers.

As he walked to the door, Ben got up and headed into the bathroom. "See you shortly."

BEN STOOD at the door to Rob's suite and rang the doorbell. After a couple of moments, Rob opened the door and invited Ben in, planting a quick peck on his cheek, then asked, "Have you heard of the Bluefin Bistro? It's a suite-only restaurant on Deck 15."

"No, I haven't. Is that where you want to go for breakfast?"

"Yeah, I called and they had space, so I made a reservation for us if that's okay? I thought it might be less hectic than the buffet or the Cove Café."

"That sounds great. Are you ready to go?"

"One sec. I gotta put on my wristband and grab my phone." Rob turned and went into the bedroom.

As they made their way to the restaurant, Ben said, "The ship seems quiet today. Did everyone sleep in or something?"

"Actually, we docked in Genoa a couple of hours ago. Most folks were probably up early and are already off on shore excursions or something."

"Ah, that's right. But you're not planning on going anyway, right?"

"No. I actually love staying on the ship when we're in port somewhere. There are hardly any people around and it kind of feels like the ship is mine to enjoy. Besides, I've been to Genoa before and while I enjoyed it, I didn't feel the need to go back this time."

They arrived at the bistro and were seated near a window overlooking the dock area. It was a beautiful sunny day, and they could see people walking about in the city. There were a few other occupied tables in the restaurant, but it wasn't crowded at all.

The restaurant was bright and airy, with sleek wood accents. The walls were off-white, and the linens were pale sage and cream. A small silver vase with orange flowers sat in the center of each table. It was a beautiful space that once again reflected a calm serenity that could be felt in many parts of the ship.

A server approached their table with a carafe and asked if they wanted coffee. After pouring a cup for each of them, they set the carafe down on the table and took their breakfast order.

"You said that they serve dinner here too, right?" Ben asked.

"Yes. Why?"

"I think I'd like to come back here for dinner one night. In fact, do you have any plans for dinner tonight, Rob?" Ben asked slyly, with a crooked grin.

Rob made a point of quickly checking the calendar on his phone and then peered into Ben's eyes, "As a matter of fact, I don't. Are you asking me to dine with you this evening?"

Ben beamed. "Yes I am."

"I'd love to have dinner with you tonight. And the Suite Lounge is directly opposite from here. We could have a drink there before dinner."

"Excellent. I'll speak with the hostess when we leave and see if we can get a reservation for tonight."

The server returned with their food. Waffles with fresh

strawberries and crisp bacon for Rob, and a ham and cheese omelet with hash brown potatoes for Ben.

They ate in silence, enjoying their food and the company.

"More coffee?" Ben asked as he picked up the carafe. Rob nodded and Ben topped off each cup.

Rob sipped his coffee. "Do you have any plans for today, Ben?"

"Not really. I'll probably just find a quiet spot and read for a while. What about you?"

"It's a beautiful day. I thought perhaps I'd get a little exercise. There's a walking and jogging track on Deck 17; a few laps would do me good. Then I think I'll sit out on my balcony and read. You're welcome to join me if you'd like."

"I'd love to. We can stop at my cabin when we leave here so I can grab my sunglasses and Kindle."

As they left the restaurant, Ben spoke with the hostess and made a reservation for eight o'clock that night.

Ben had a thought. "We should have breakfast here tomorrow before heading off the ship, don't you think? We have to meet for the shore excursion at ten in the Ocean Theater." He turned to the hostess, "Is it possible to get a reservation for eight-thirty tomorrow morning?"

"Let me check." After tapping a few keys on her keyboard, she turned back to Ben, "You're all set, sir."

They walked to Ben's suite at a leisurely pace. A comfortable silence settled over them.

Ben felt so relaxed in Rob's company. *This feels so right.*

They had both dressed in jeans and T-shirts that morning, but Ben had worn deck shoes to breakfast. "I'm gonna change into sneakers if we're going to do laps."

Rob stepped out onto the balcony while he waited for Ben

to change his shoes and grab his things. After a moment he went back into the cabin and called out, "It's getting warm out there. You might want to bring a pair of shorts or a bathing suit with you. It will probably be nice enough to sunbathe later if you feel like it."

"Okay, I'll grab my backpack and get everything together. Which reminds me, I really like that mini-pack that you have. Where did you get it?"

"I found it online. I'll search for it later and send you a link."

"Thanks." Ben walked out of the bedroom with his backpack slung over his shoulder. "Okay, let's go."

A COUPLE of other people were walking on the track when they got up to the Sun Deck, but thankfully, it wasn't at all crowded. They walked at a good pace, raising their heart rate a bit, but not overdoing it. Though neither of them spoke, the silence wasn't awkward or unpleasant.

After about fifteen minutes Rob said, "One more lap and I think I'm done." A sheen of sweat glistened on his forehead. "It's warmer than I thought up here."

"Yeah, it is," Ben agreed. "I'm glad you suggested I bring a bathing suit with me. I definitely want to change when we get to your cabin."

After the last lap, they walked away from the jogging track and leaned against the ship's railing to cool down a bit. "I feel better about having waffles and bacon for breakfast this morning."

"You're not overweight, Rob."

Rob blushed. "Oh, I know, but if I ate like that all the time and *didn't* exercise, it wouldn't be pretty."

"Yeah, I get it. I've never really had a weight problem, but I do find that I need to exercise a bit more as I get older."

"Same. At home I have an elliptical machine and I try to get on that three or four times a week. I'm not trying to lose weight, I just don't want to gain."

When they got to Rob's cabin, he pointed toward the guest bathroom and said, "Make yourself at home."

Rob headed for the master bathroom, stopping to pull his bathing suit out of a drawer on the way.

He freshened up and changed, then grabbed his Kindle, phone, and sunglasses and went out onto the balcony. There was a small cabinet on the side containing some large beach towels; he pulled out two, placing them on the lounge chairs with a table between them.

Ben appeared at the sliding doors and Rob looked at him, admiring Ben's hairy chest and the fur trail that disappeared below the waistband of his swimsuit. Ben's suit was form-fitting trunks similar to his own. But his was a gray-to-black stripe in an ombre effect while Ben's was a bright bottle-green that bulged nicely in the front. Clearing his now dry throat, he asked, "Can you grab a couple of bottles of water out of the fridge, please?"

"Sure, I'll be right back."

Rob couldn't help but notice how the suit snugly cupped Ben's ass when he turned to get the water. *Give me strength!*

They sat quietly reading and listening to the music coming from the Pool Deck. It was warm, but not overly so; a gentle breeze kept them both comfortable. Before they knew it, a couple of hours had passed in companionable silence.

Rob stretched and checked the time on his phone. "I was thinking of ordering something for lunch. Are you hungry?"

Ben's stomach chose that moment to growl.

Rob laughed and Ben joined in. "I guess that's your answer!"

Rob fetched the room service menu. Handing it to Ben he said, "I'll be right back. Nature calls."

When he returned, Ben got up and said, "My turn." Before he left for the bathroom he added, "I'll have the mixed green salad with grilled salmon, please."

Rob quickly perused the menu and decided on the salad with spicy grilled shrimp. He called room service, adding a bottle of Pinot Grigio to the order.

When the food arrived, Rob asked the server to set it up on the balcony table. They ate alfresco and people-watched, admiring a few good-looking guys at the pool.

When they finished eating, Ben picked up the plates and went inside, placing the dishes on the bar in the dining area. The cabin attendant would remove them when they checked the suite later to replace towels and turn down the bed.

Rob picked up the wine bottle and glasses and followed, settling on the sofa.

"There's something I wanted to ask you, Ben," he said seriously.

"Hmm, that sounds a bit ominous," Ben replied, narrowing his eyes. "But sure, what do you want to ask?"

"Well, do you remember the night we first kissed at the hotel in Barcelona, and you told me you thought you might be demi?" Rob paused, thinking about how to phrase this next part.

"I do," Ben said, encouraging Rob to continue.

"You said you wanted to go out with me again. In fact, we both said that we wanted to see each other again. But what about your career? I don't remember ever seeing anything about your personal life in the news. I'm not really comfortable hiding who I am but I also don't want to put you in a weird position. I mean, it's not my place to tell you that you have to come out for me or anything. Argh! I think I'm getting all this wrong. Do you understand what I'm trying to say?"

Ben's smile was sweet when he gazed at Rob. "I know exactly what you mean. And it's not as bad or weird or whatever as what you have spinning around in your head.

"Look, I haven't really done a big Hollywood blockbuster in about five years. And much of that was my choice. I'm getting older and I want to slow down. The last two films I did were indies and that's what I want to focus on more. I made enough money early on in my career and I think I invested pretty wisely, so while I'm not a multibillionaire or anything, I'm very comfortable."

"But you don't want to stop acting, do you?" Rob asked.

"No, but I want to work on other projects. I've had a couple of offers to do something on Broadway and that's definitely an avenue I want to pursue. When I get back to LA, I have a meeting with my agent during which I fully intend to talk about what's next for me. And if it's okay with you, I'd like to tell her about you and how I hope to have you in my life a lot more."

"Really?" Rob looked at him, surprised. "You really want me in your life? You're sure?"

"Oh yeah, I'm sure. These last few days have been amazing. But what about you, how do you feel about having me in your life?" Ben asked shyly. "Is this too soon for you? The last thing I want to do is make you feel uncomfortable."

Rob shook his head. "First of all, yesterday was more of a shit-show than anything else and I'm sorry about that. But it also made me realize—well, after I had my meltdown moment and cried on Sam's virtual shoulder for a while—that I am ready to move on. And that dream, or whatever it was when Alan and I talked, well that really hit home, too. You made me realize that there's something here between us and I'd be an idiot to ignore it. So yes, I would love to have you in my life more."

He paused and then a thought occurred that made his eyes widen, "Oh, my God, if you do get something on Broadway, that means New York, right? You'd only be a few hours away!"

"Exactly!" Ben replied, clearly excited about the prospect. "That's one of the things I thought about yesterday when you were having your crisis. And I'm happy to hear that you admit that even though yesterday was a tough day, something good did come out of it."

"I am too," Rob agreed.

"I was also thinking about doing a bit more research into demisexuality," Ben continued. "In the past, my relationships developed over time. What you and I have all happened pretty quickly, so I guess what I'm saying is that I don't know what I am—bi, demi, something else entirely maybe."

"I don't really think it matters, Ben. I'm not a big fan of labels, anyway. You're 'you' and I like you. Isn't that the important thing?"

Ben reached out and took Rob's hand. "Yes, you're right. Labels be damned. They're not as important as what you and I are feeling." Ben admitted. "And I like you too. A lot. As much as I want to walk around the ship holding hands with you, I'm gonna wait until I talk to Amanda, my agent, so that she doesn't have to find out I have a boyfriend from the tabloids. Is that okay?"

"Boyfriend, huh?" Rob grinned widely. "I like the sound of that. And yes, we can wait until you talk to Amanda. But after you tell her, I plan on holding the hell outta your hand in public, okay?"

"Absolutely." They leaned into each other and kissed. It started slow, Ben kissing him gently on his mouth, his jaw, his neck. Then it grew hot, their tongues dueling. Rob sucked on Ben's tongue, moaning.

"As much as I want more of you Ben," Rob said, breathless, "can we just take this a little slowly? I really do want you, please believe that Ben. I just need to pace myself a bit. Is that okay?" *Because I'd feel like a fifteen-year-old if I came in my shorts right now.*

Ben panted. "Yeah, I understand. I really do want you too, but I'll wait until you're ready. I don't wanna do anything to fuck this up."

They kissed a few more times, keeping it soft and gentle. When they finally separated, they both tried to inconspicuously adjust themselves. Catching each other, they both giggled.

"When we do finally go for more, it's gonna be an inferno, isn't it?" Rob asked.

"You know it!"

A little while later, Ben changed and said he was going to head back to his own cabin. "I'll pick you up for dinner around seven so we have time for a drink in the Suite Lounge before our reservation."

CHAPTER 10

The evening had been wonderful. They began with drinks in the Suite Lounge, a vodka martini for Rob, a manhattan for Ben.

Dinner was great. They chose oysters for an appetizer, then Rob decided on roasted branzino for his entree while Ben selected the cioppino. They shared a bottle of Sauvignon Blanc and skipped dessert.

Walking around the Pool Deck after dinner, Rob asked, "Would you like to get a nightcap and take it back to my cabin? We can sit on the balcony and relax a bit."

"Yeah, that would be nice."

They stopped at the next bar they passed and, with drinks in hand, made their way up to Rob's suite.

They sat in relative silence, sipping their drinks and holding hands. Finally, Rob said, "This is my favorite time of day on a ship. Whatever else I do during the day, whether it's spending time in port somewhere or just hanging out on the ship, I love sitting on my balcony with a drink at the end of the day and just relaxing. Thank you for being here with me, Ben."

"Thanks for inviting me. I can't think of anywhere else I'd rather be." He squeezed Rob's hand and smiled.

Before they knew it, their drinks were empty and it was getting late. They had to be up in time for breakfast and their excursion to Tuscania in the morning.

Rob walked Ben to the door and hugged him tightly. They kissed deeply but stopped before things got too heated and said their good nights. "I'll call you in the morning, Rob."

Tuesday, October 8 - Civitavecchia and aboard Ocean Wanderer

Ben woke just before his alarm went off. He slept well, but dreamed of Rob in his bed, kissing and frotting against each other until they both came. He had a serious case of morning wood that he knew he'd have to deal with in the shower.

Not wasting another moment, he shut off the alarm and walked into the bathroom. He wouldn't be able to pee in this condition, so he turned on the shower and waited a moment for the water to warm up. Stepping under the spray, he grabbed the shower gel and squirted some into his hand.

He touched himself, stroking gently to start. As the lather

built up, he cupped his balls with his other hand and squeezed gently. Moaning, he closed his eyes and thought of Rob in that tight swimsuit yesterday, how it clung to his ass. Just a few more strokes and he painted the wall of the shower with his seed.

What am I, thirteen? I can't remember the last time I did something like that, but I really needed to take the edge off.

Sighing, he finished showering, rinsing the wall so that he didn't leave any trace of his earlier activity.

Once he was dressed, he texted Rob.

R U awake?

A couple of moments passed and then.

Yes, just got out of the shower. R U ready?

Yeah, but it's too early to go to breakfast.

OK, come to my room for coffee.

Ben chuckled. He put on his shoes and stuck his phone in his pocket. Putting on his wristband, he headed out.

Rob answered his door, holding a cup of coffee. "This will cost you one kiss, please," he said, smiling. He was shirtless and wearing jeans that weren't quite zipped all the way.

"Gladly." Ben leaned in and kissed him. "Good morning. Is it too soon for me to call you sweetheart?"

"Not at all." Rob grabbed his own cup and toasted, "Here's to boyfriends and sweethearts."

"You're in a very good mood today."

"I am!" Rob exclaimed, not bothering to hide how happy he was feeling. "I had a wonderful day yesterday and slept great last night. And now we're going on an adventure today. I'm very excited about spending the day with you."

They sat and sipped their coffee.

"I woke up kind of early today and took out my journal. I made some entries about the first few days of this trip. It actually felt good to sit and write things down. Yeah, it *was* bittersweet in some ways, but nothing I couldn't handle. I'm glad I did it. I'm sure it'll be easier next time."

"I'm really proud of you, Rob. That couldn't have been easy." Ben reached out and took his hand. "You're amazing."

"Thanks. Since we've talked things through over the past couple of days, I'm really feeling calm about everything now. I know that I won't ever forget Alan, and part of me will always love him, but I finally feel that I'm ready to move forward. You've helped me see that."

"I don't want you to forget Alan. He was an important part of your life for a long time. He's part of you. Do you think there's room for both of us in your heart?"

"Yeah, I know there is." Rob moved toward Ben and kissed him soundly. "Now let me grab a shirt and then we can go eat."

AFTER BREAKFAST, they returned to their respective cabins to freshen up and retrieve their backpacks. They met outside the Ocean Theater on Deck 6 and went in together.

They sat and waited, listening to other groups get called. Finally, after fifteen or twenty minutes, their group was directed out through a different door. They followed a staff member down a few sets of stairs, through security, and off the ship to a waiting bus.

Once everyone was onboard and seated, the tour guide introduced herself and the driver before departing.

It was a pleasant ride through the stunning Italian countryside to Tuscania. The day was sunny and the sky was a rich blue with a few puffy clouds. Within forty minutes they arrived at their first destination.

"You'll have an hour and a half here to explore on your own," the tour guide explained. She spoke with a lovely Italian accent, but her English was quite good, and they had no trouble understanding her. "I have maps for you to take as you leave the bus. Worth seeing are the Basilica of San Pietro and the Tower of Lavello. Also, the *Fontana delle Sette Cannelle* is a medieval fountain; it's a great spot for a photo."

"This place sounds incredible. I can't wait to see it all with you," Ben whispered.

"The countryside is very picturesque," the tour guide continued. "There are shops and cafés along the main street, as well. It is now just eleven o'clock, so please be back here by twelve-thirty and we will go to the Giorgio Farm for a brief tour and then lunch. *Grazie.*"

They got off the bus and took a look at the map. Deciding to skip the church, they set off for the tower and both agreed that the fountain was high on both their lists of things to see.

They wandered around slowly, stopping for an espresso at a café they passed and looking in a few shops. The town dated to medieval times and they appreciated the architecture, taking photos of doors and buildings along the way. The fountain really was beautiful, the square where it was situated was at the end of the main street. It overlooked the countryside, and the view was breathtaking. They took lots of photos, including a few selfies.

"I feel like just an average tourist," Ben said. "No one seems to recognize me. I love it."

He had worn a baseball cap and sunglasses which made him less recognizable, but still felt natural, and that didn't happen as often as he would've liked.

"I'm so happy to be on this cruise, but more importantly, I'm happy I met you and that we can share this time together."

"Me, too," Rob agreed. "Every day is better than the last."

They walked around a bit more then slowly made their way back to the bus. There had been only one other tour bus there when they arrived, and it was gone when they got back to their bus.

Rob checked his watch and saw they were early, so they sat on a nearby bench and did a bit of people-watching while they waited. After some time, they boarded the bus and took their seats.

The rest of the passengers all made it back in time, and they departed promptly. "Thank you all for coming back to the bus on time," the tour guide said. "I've spoken with someone at the farm; we will have lunch as soon as we get there, followed by a short tour. We should arrive at the farm in about ten minutes."

When the bus arrived at the Giorgio Farm, they were led into a large tent. There were round tables set up, each with eight chairs. Ben and Rob chose a table and were soon joined by six fellow tourists.

There were pitchers of water and bottles of red wine on the table. Servers brought out trays of olives and cheese along with baskets of thickly sliced rustic bread and bottles of olive oil. Everyone helped themselves to the food and drink and chatted casually.

Phil and Simone were an older couple from Washington State who spoke enthusiastically about how much they were enjoying the cruise so far. They too were continuing on the next cruise across the Atlantic.

Melissa and Don were a bit younger and had cruised a couple of times before, but this was their first time in Europe and the transatlantic would be a new experience for them. They lived in Florida, just outside of Fort Lauderdale.

Melissa asked if Rob and Ben had traveled much. "This is only my second cruise," Ben said, "And unfortunately I'm leaving in a few days when we arrive back in Barcelona. But I'm enjoying this so much and definitely want to do it again."

"I've cruised a lot," Rob stated. "I think this is number thirty-seven or thirty-eight for me. And I'm continuing on for the transatlantic as well. In fact, a friend of mine is flying into Barcelona in a couple of days and is joining me on the next cruise."

"Oh," Melissa looked surprised, "I thought the two of you were together."

"We actually just met a couple of days before the cruise," Ben responded. "We were staying at the same hotel and started chatting at the bar one afternoon."

"Yeah, when we learned we'd both be on the cruise, we decided to hang out together since we were both traveling alone," added Rob.

Simone looked at Ben and said, "Pardon me, but you look awfully familiar. Have we ever met before?"

"I don't believe so, but you may have seen me somewhere. I'm Ben Rockingham."

"Oh, of course, that's it!" Phil joined in. "We've seen your films. It's very nice to meet you." He reached over to shake Ben's hand.

"Thank you. I appreciate it, but if it's all the same to you, I'd prefer to keep a low profile on the trip." Ben smiled sweetly. "Just trying to relax for a few days before I head back to the States."

The remaining couple at their table appeared a bit older and had introduced themselves as Sarah and Jerry but hadn't said much more than that.

The servers returned with large bowls of pasta covered in steaming tomato sauce and freshly grated cheese. They set them on the tables along with a stack of small bowls so that everyone could help themselves. They also replenished the water and bottles of wine as they were emptied.

Serving themselves and each other, Rob and Ben dug into the flavorful food.

As they ate, an older gentleman walked to the front of the dining area. He was dressed in simple work clothes. His hair was graying a bit, but his bright blue eyes were filled with pride. It was clear that he was the head of this family business. "Good afternoon everyone, I am Antonio Giorgio. This farm has been in my family for three generations. After lunch, we will go on a short tour." He spoke with a heavy Italian accent.

"That sounds like fun," Ben remarked.

"I wanted to tell you that the olives you enjoyed earlier came from our olive groves and the grapes to make the wine you are drinking were also grown here. We also grew the tomatoes used in the sauce for your pasta today. And for dessert, there will be cake spread with cherry preserves that comes from our cherry orchards. We hope you are enjoying everything. *Buon appetito!*"

Everyone applauded when he finished. The tour guide standing off to the side said, "There are toilet facilities around to the back if anyone needs them. Once you are finished with dessert, please meet back outside for the tour. It is only a little bit of walking but if anyone wants to skip that, our driver will be near the bus and you can get back on whenever you'd like."

Trays of cake were delivered to the tables and folks continued to chat among themselves as they finished lunch.

When they finally headed out of the tent for the tour, Ben turned to Rob, "I'm so happy you asked me to join you for this. I've had such a good time. Thank you."

"Of course. While I'm sure I would've had a enjoyed this by myself, it's a lot more fun with someone else. I'm really glad you're here with me."

The tour was, indeed, short. They walked around a bit and saw the olive groves and the main garden area where the tomatoes and a wide assortment of vegetables were grown. In the distance, they could see the cherry orchards. There was a small stand on the side where the Giorgio family sold olive oil, wine, and cherry preserves.

Rob and Ben each bought a few jars of the preserves. "I'm not much for souvenirs," Rob said. "But I'll enjoy this at breakfast when I get home and remember the time I spent here with you."

CHAPTER 11

Tuesday, October 8 - Aboard *Ocean Wanderer*, later the same day

Back on the ship, as Ben and Rob walked along the Promenade Deck, Rob said, "I know we agreed to spend time together on the cruise, and so far we've been pretty inseparable. But if you need some alone-time, please tell me. You said this trip was a time for you to relax; I'll give you some space if you want."

"Are you kidding?" Ben scoffed. "I'm having such a good time hanging out with you. I want to spend all my time with you, if that's okay."

Rob was relieved. "Okay, good. Just my way of keeping the lines of communication open. I want to hang out with you, too. Now that we've agreed on that, what do you want to do for dinner tonight?"

Ben grinned, looking thoughtful. "I dunno. What are my options?"

"Well, we've already eaten at the steakhouse and the Bluefin Bistro. What about Asian? There's a restaurant called Kaiyo at Seaside Cove. The name means 'ocean' by the way. They have a sushi and noodle bar along with a teppanyaki room where they cook at your table."

"I love teppanyaki, Ben told Rob, "but it seems like a bit too much food for tonight. Lunch was pretty filling. But I would definitely be interested in sushi and perhaps some noodles."

"That's perfect, Ben. Let me see if I can make a reservation."

He pulled up the ship's app on his phone but apparently could only make a reservation for himself since he was the only guest registered in his cabin. He told Ben he couldn't do it in the app and they walked over to the Guest Services desk, since they were heading in that direction anyway. He explained the situation to Roberto, who was assisting him. Roberto called Kaiyo and was able to make a reservation for the two of them for eight-thirty that evening.

They went to Ben's cabin and talked about what to do next. It was almost four-thirty, so they had plenty of time before their reservation.

"I think I'd like to take a short nap," Rob said. He paused, hoping what he said next would sound light and a bit playful. "Would you like to come to my suite and take a nap with me?" He smiled shyly at Ben.

"Are you sure?"

"Yeah. I was thinking you could bring a change of clothes with you. We can nap and then freshen up and change before dinner. And we'll probably have time if you wanted to get a drink at the Suite Lounge before dinner, too."

Ben smiled, making Rob's stomach flutter with excitement. "That sounds wonderful. Let me put a few things together."

As Ben quickly tossed a few items into his backpack, Rob's heart raced. He was nervous—*this is my first time since Alan*—but the nerves were from excitement, not fear. He wanted this... desperately.

"Okay, I'm ready."

When they got to his suite, Rob took the hangers from Ben and hung them in his closet. He set an alarm on his phone for six-thirty and placed it on the nightstand.

Toeing off his sneakers, he took off his shirt and jeans. Ben smiled, obviously enjoying the view.

"Are you going to join me?" Rob teased.

Ben quickly undressed and they slid under the covers. Ben looked into Rob's eyes, "I don't want you to do anything you're not comfortable with, Rob. You take the lead and I'll follow."

Rob moved closer, hugging him. When their chests touched, Rob sighed. *Oh my God, I've missed this feeling so much.* "You feel so good."

Rob claimed his mouth, running his tongue along Ben's lips and pressing forward. Ben opened to him and they kissed long and hard, taking turns probing and sucking. Rob's hands glided down Ben's back. When he reached the waistband of Ben's briefs, he slipped one hand in, cupping Ben's ass cheek and squeezing lightly. He moaned into Ben's mouth.

Ben followed suit, dipping both hands into Rob's underwear, massaging his ass and pulling him closer. They were both rock hard and Ben could feel his cock leaking.

Rob reached down and touched Ben's cock through his shorts. Ben whimpered and Rob could feel the head of Ben's cock poke up from the waistband. He swiped his thumb over the slit and shuddered at the feel of precum leaking out.

He brought his thumb up to his mouth and licked it.

"Oh fuck," Ben sighed. "I need to taste you. Please?"

Rob nodded as Ben lowered the covers and slid down, kissing Rob's chest, teasing a nipple and working his way down. He tongued Rob's navel and continued lower. He mouthed Rob's cock through his briefs and then grasped the waistband and lowered them. Rob's cock popped out and slapped his belly. His cock was long and not too thick, a good six inches.

Ben licked up the length and sucked in the head, swirling his tongue around the crown of Rob's cock.

"Slow down or this is gonna be over way too quick," Rob panted. "Fuck, please!' he pleaded.

Ben backed off and let Rob catch his breath. When Rob's breathing slowed a bit, Ben took Rob's cock all the way to the back of his throat, his nose buried in Rob's pubic hair. He pulled off, then moved back up to kiss Rob deeply.

Rob moaned into the kiss, feeling so good that he'd taken this next step. He needed this connection with someone—it *had* been too long. Ben was definitely good for him.

Rob lowered Ben's shorts and grabbed his hard cock again. It was hot and slick in his hand as he moved up and down the length, cupping Ben's balls with his other hand. He swiped his thumb over the slit again and, gathering up the precum there, he slicked Ben's cock and jerked him again.

Looking at Ben with a wicked grin, Rob moved down and around so that they were each mouth-to-cock. Rob buried his nose in the space between Ben's thigh and balls and inhaled deeply, relishing Ben's scent. It was intoxicating. He drew one testicle into his mouth and sucked lightly, then drew his tongue up Ben's rigid cock. Rob thought they were about the same length, but Ben was definitely thicker. He sucked Ben's cockhead and pushed lower, taking as much as he could.

Ben sucked lightly on the head of Rob's cock, occasionally moving farther down until he swallowed the entire length. He trailed a finger behind Rob's balls and stroked him slowly until he reached his pucker. He circled the ring of muscle lightly with the pad of his finger. Rob groaned.

Rob pulled off Ben's cock and panted, "Fuck, I'm gonna come!"

Ben sped up, caressing his hole and sucking Rob's cock into his throat. Rob's orgasm shook him and he could feel his com hitting the back of Ben's throat.

"Ugnh!" Rob grunted, lips still wrapped around the head of Ben's dick. He lightly tugged Ben's balls and heard a moan. Then Ben was coming and Rob did his best to swallow, but a bit dribbled out of the side of his mouth.

When their breathing slowed, Rob moved back around, "Oh my God!"

"Yeah," Ben agreed. "That was amazing."

They kissed, tasting each other, and Ben licked at the side of Rob's mouth, cleaning away his cum. Rob turned over and they spooned, completely satisfied. Rob sighed and snuggled closer. He couldn't remember the last time he felt that content. Before long, they were both asleep.

THEY WOKE to the sound of an alarm. Rob reached for his phone to shut it off, and Ben gently pulled him back into a spooning hug.

"Hi," he whispered into Rob's ear. "Are you okay?"

"Hi yourself. And yes, I'm better than okay. I can't really explain it, but this feels so perfect."

Ben moved his hips and his dick nestled along Rob's ass crack.

"Don't start anything, Ben," Rob sighed but Ben could tell he was smiling. "We have to get cleaned up before dinner."

"Okay, fine." He smirked, wishing they could just stay in bed. But he knew that Rob was right—there would be time for other things later.

Ben rose from the bed, tugging his boxer briefs from between his knees with a chuckle. He tossed them on the floor and headed for the bathroom. He stood at the toilet and peed. He hadn't closed the door, so Rob walked in and turned the faucet in the shower. The glass-enclosed shower was definitely large enough for both of them, so Rob turned to Ben asking, "Join me?"

They showered together, lathering each other's slippery bodies and exchanging sloppy wet kisses, but managed to not get carried away. Stepping out of the shower, they dried off and Ben looked around for his backpack.

"I think you left it on a chair in the dining room," Rob told him.

Ben retrieved his deodorant and toothbrush and returned to the bathroom. "I forgot my comb. Mind if I borrow yours?" he asked.

"I don't think I have a comb, but there should be a brush in my shaving kit."

As they finished dressing, Ben peered at Rob, "I've been thinking. I want to tell Amanda about us now, if that's okay with you. I know I said I was gonna wait until I got back to the States, but then Simone recognized me yesterday and I'm pretty sure a few folks on the ship have as well. No one has come up to me or anything, but I've seen a few people stare and nod when I notice them, like they know who I am."

"Oh Ben, I'm sorry if I did…"

"No, it's totally fine. I don't care if people recognize me and I don't care if people assume something about us. I just think it might be better to tell Amanda now, just in case something gets back to her. Is that okay?" he asked again.

"Of course it is. Do you want to call her now?"

"Yeah, it will only take a few minutes."

"Sure, I'll be out on the balcony," Rob said, pecking Ben's cheek. "Take your time."

A few minutes later, Ben joined him out on the balcony.

"How'd it go?"

"Fine. She admitted that she thought I might be bi, and she really didn't care. Then she said, and I quote, 'It's about fucking time you found someone, Ben,' which made me laugh. She doesn't pull any punches that one. I think I mentioned it before, but I believe she and Sam would get along really well."

"Actually, you were talking about your assistant before, and I think all three of them would get along. But the bigger question is which would be worse—do we introduce them or do our damnedest to keep them apart?" Rob laughed.

"Introduce them, I think. They all really just want the best for us. Then Amanda told me to do whatever the hell I wanted, and she'd deal with any rumors that might crop up. We'll talk more when I see her in about a week, but she doesn't think this will have any impact on my career."

Rob squeezed Ben's hand. "Whew, I'm happy to hear that. I'd hate to think that what's happened between us could affect you negatively."

"I'm sure it'll all be fine. If Amanda isn't worried, then I'm not. The only thing we'll need to decide fairly quickly is if we just go about our business and let things be known when folks catch wind of it, or if I make some sort of statement about it. Either a press release or a post on social media, something that presents us as a couple." Ben paused, his brain spinning with decisions. "But we don't need to think about that now. C'mon, Rob. Let's go get a drink before dinner."

THE SUITE LOUNGE wasn't very crowded. They grabbed two seats at the end of the bar nearest the windows so they could look out over the water. The ship had left Civitavecchia around six o'clock, and the sun had set shortly after that, but it was still beautiful to watch the sea at twilight.

After they ordered drinks, Ben asked the bartender why it wasn't very busy in the lounge. Since it was only open until eight-thirty for drinks, he expected to see more people.

"Ah well, many of the passengers staying in the suites are older, so they come for a drink or two around five o'clock when we open. After that, they go to dinner and then to the early show," the bartender explained.

"That works out well for us then," Ben replied. "I like it when it's less crowded."

They sipped their martinis and chatted a bit.

"So, Ben, I know you're getting off the cruise on Saturday and I really don't want to think about that yet, but I do have a question for you."

"I don't want to think about it either, but sure, what do you want to know?"

"What time is your flight back to LA?" Rob asked.

"Actually, I'm not leaving until Sunday morning. I have an eight o'clock flight. Why?"

"Well, Sam's flying into Barcelona on Thursday and is playing tourist on Friday," Rob explained. "I told her I would meet her at the hotel on Saturday. She's staying at the L17 like we did. I was thinking that maybe you and I can meet outside at the pier on Saturday to grab a taxi to the hotel and you could meet Sam. Maybe we'd have time for lunch or something?"

"I can do you one better," Ben replied. "I have a car picking me up at the pier. And I'm staying at that hotel again for one night. That means you can join me in the car, and we'll head to the hotel. I'll check in, then I can meet Sam and we'll definitely have lunch together. I'll see if I can get a reservation at the seafood restaurant you and I dined at the night before the cruise. After lunch, I can have the car drop you back at the pier."

"That would be awesome," Rob said, excited at the prospect of spending more time with Ben. "Plus, you and I get an extra day together."

"Then that's what we're gonna do."

They finished their drinks and headed down to Kaiyo on Deck 8.

They checked in and were seated at the sushi and noodle

bar in the restaurant. They shared some spicy tuna roll, pork gyoza and tempura shrimp as an appetizer. They also got spicy miso ramen bowls with char siu pork. "This meal was amazing," Ben declared as they finished dinner. "Everything is so flavorful and well prepared. The food on this ship seems much better than what I remember from my last cruise."

"Yes," Rob agreed. "Most of the cruise lines have upped their game with the addition of specialty restaurants. They're cooking for fewer people than in the main dining rooms, so the quality is definitely elevated."

After dinner they were walking along Seaside Cove and stopped at the Trident Lounge for a nightcap. Lukas was working at the bar and he welcomed them and took their order. Rather than remain seated at the bar, they took their drinks and sat at a table close to the walkway. They sipped their bourbon and people-watched.

Rob sighed, "How is it that I met you less than a week ago, but I feel like I've known you forever?"

"I think we were just meant to be, Rob. Let's not question it. Just accept it and enjoy it."

"That's a very good plan," Rob decided. He paused, trying not to look nervous. "So, will you stay with me tonight, Ben? Don't get me wrong. I'm not a horndog looking for more sex or anything, but I do enjoy being with you and I really, really hate sleeping alone."

Ben laughed. Rob noticed how his eyes sparkled when he laughed; Ben's face lit up and he was even more handsome. "I'd like that. A lot."

CHAPTER 12

Wednesday, October 9 - At sea aboard *Ocean Wanderer*

Rob opened his eyes. He smiled as he realized his arms were wrapped around Ben and he couldn't believe how good it felt. It was mostly dark in the bedroom, but he could tell it was morning as a bit of light peeked out from between the drapes. He listened to Ben's even breathing and assumed he must still be asleep.

I'm so lucky I met him. And I'm even luckier that he's interested in me. He always seems calm and even-tempered. Kinda like the yin to my yang. The way he handled my meltdown, he never got angry or upset. He just listened and took care of me. Ben is exactly what I need. I hope we can continue this...relationship, I guess is the right word. We already agreed we're boyfriends. I think I'm way over my head already and I don't think I could stop seeing him if I wanted to.

He breathed contentedly and ran his fingers through Ben's chest hair. "Good morning, Rob," Ben said sleepily, then he pushed his ass into Rob's crotch.

Ben turned over and hugged Rob before kissing him soundly. They were both wearing underwear, but that didn't stop them from rubbing together a bit as they kissed.

"God, you feel good." Rob cooed.

"Mmmm, you do too." Rob's stomach growled and they both giggled.

"So, breakfast instead of blowjobs, right?" Ben asked, smiling cheekily.

"We don't really have plans for today, so maybe blowjobs later?" Rob joked. "But yeah, breakfast now, please."

They cleaned up in record time and decided on the Cove Café for their morning meal as that would be pretty quick. After making their selections, they sat outside and ate bagels and cream cheese, yogurt with fruit and granola, and coffee.

"Feel better?" Ben teased after Rob finished eating.

He groaned, leaned back, and patted his stomach. "Yes, I do. Now, it's not that I think about food all the time, but would you be interested in going to Neptune's wine bar later? It opens at four o'clock and we could have some wine and tapas. And then maybe have a late dinner?"

Ben looked at him and chuckled, "I know you don't think only of food, I believe you think about sexy times, too."

Rob lowered his eyes and blushed.

"Relax, I'm only teasing you." Ben said. "And wine and tapas followed by a late dinner sounds wonderful. If you haven't figured it out yet, I'm pretty happy doing anything as long as we can be together."

"I'm glad," Rob admitted, "because I plan on hanging out

with you as much as I can. And now that I've eaten, I need to move. C'mon, let's walk."

They started out walking around Seaside Cove for a while, but Rob really wanted to pick up the pace a bit, so they headed up to the jogging track. Not that they planned on jogging, but at least there they could walk at a good pace and feel like they were actually exercising.

"I know another way we could get our heart rate up, you know," Ben offered with a sexy grin.

"Ha! Now who has sexy times on the brain, huh?" teased Rob. "All in good time, my dear. All in good time."

Twenty minutes later, Ben stopped and looked for a place to sit. "That's it, I'm done. I'm not as young as I used to be."

"Hey, I've got three years on you, old man!" Rob joked, but he gladly sat as well.

"I'm just saving myself for later," Ben replied, waggling his eyebrows.

They headed back to Rob's cabin and Ben collected his stuff. "I don't have any clean clothes here, and after that little workout I really need another shower. What do you want to do between now and tapas?"

"It's really nice out. We could relax in the sun and read for a bit and then maybe hit the hot tub in a little while. How does that sound?"

"That sounds wonderful, Rob. I'll be back in a little while."

"Bring some extra clothes with you if you'd like," Rob suggested, his eyes bright. "But no pressure."

"You're just full of excellent ideas today, sweetheart." Ben chuckled warmly.

Rob grinned widely at the endearment. "Hurry back."

THEY READ and sunbathed for a couple of hours. The day was a bit cooler, but the glass panels surrounding the balcony blocked the worst of the breeze coming off the water, so they were quite comfortable there.

Ben put down his Kindle and sighed, "Another one that I didn't figure out."

"Your book? Oh, were you reading a mystery?"

"Yeah, Amanda got me hooked on cozy mysteries a couple of years ago and sometimes I figure it out before the big reveal, sometimes I don't. Do you read mysteries?" Ben asked.

"I do, actually. I read a lot of different things, but really enjoy mysteries. Especially thriller-types with lots of action. And if I can find one with gay characters, that's even better. But I do read cozies now and again, too. Which series are you reading?"

"It's called Cozy Corgi Mysteries by Mildred Abbott. There are quite a few out and it looks like the author doesn't plan on ending anytime soon."

"Oh cool. I'll pick up the first one and see if I like it. Thanks."

"Sure," Ben replied. "You mentioned something about the hot tub earlier. Do you feel like soaking a bit?"

"That's a great idea. I checked it earlier and it should be good to go. Can you grab a couple of towels from the cabinet and put them on that chair, please?"

Rob hit the switch that turned on the hot tub jets and they climbed in. The warm water was like heaven on his skin. Ben moaned and grabbed Rob's hand.

"This feels amazing. I think I need more hot-tub time in my life."

"Me too." Rob agreed. "I've been thinking about putting one in at home. I'm definitely gonna find a contractor when I get back. I'll have to ask Sam if she knows anyone."

"Oooh, more incentive for me to pay you a visit, huh?"

"You're welcome to visit me anytime, but if putting in a hot tub gets you there faster, I promise to get it done quickly, although spring is probably the earliest it can be installed. I have a tiered deck in the back of the house; I'll need to figure out the best place for the tub."

"Nice. Is it a big house?" Ben asked.

"It's a good-sized home. Living room, dining room, family room, office, half-bath, and large eat-in kitchen on the first floor. The second floor has a master bedroom suite with a private bath, two guest rooms that share another bathroom, and a laundry room. Oh, and there's a two-car attached garage."

"It sounds great. My place in LA isn't large, but then I don't spend a lot of time there. It's a two-bedroom, two-bath, pretty much all I need. And you're also welcome to visit me anytime."

"Well then it's settled, we'll both visit each other. But now," Rob continued, looking at his hands, "if we don't get out of this hot tub, our bodies are gonna prune all over, just like my fingertips are now."

He laughed and wiggled his fingers at Ben. Sure enough, they were wrinkled, and when Ben checked his own hands, he saw they were in the same condition.

"Okay, but only if we can do this again later. I bet this is amazing in the moonlight." Ben said with a wink. He grinned widely and Rob was pretty sure Ben was thinking about more than just soaking in the hot tub.

"I'm sure we can make that work. But it's almost four o'clock, so let's dry off and go to Neptune's. And while we drink wine and try some tapas, we can talk about what to do for a late dinner."

Ben laughed and nodded. "Yes sir!"

———

BEN AND ROB entered the wine bar and were struck by how beautiful it was. Chairs and sofas upholstered with dark wood and leather gave the space an elegant atmosphere. Black-and-white photos of vineyard landscapes hung on the pale sage walls. Wall sconces and battery-operated tea lights on the tables provided a warm glow throughout the room.

A wood bar with brass rails was off to the right. The wine tender standing behind it looked at them and smiled. "Sit anywhere you'd like, gentlemen."

"May we sit at the bar?" Ben asked.

"Of course. My name is Paulo and I'm happy to serve you." They took two seats at the end of the bar and Paulo placed menus in front of them. "Wine, tapas, or both this afternoon?" he asked.

"Both," Rob replied. He scanned the menu quickly and said, "I think I'd like to try a flight, please."

Ben agreed, so they decided on two different red flights they could share. As Paulo set glasses in front of them and began to pour their wine, they perused the tapas menu. After a moment, they chose a sampler platter for two that consisted of cheese, olives, bread, and cold cuts, along with some nuts and grilled shrimp.

After pouring three samples of wine for each of them, he presented them with cards that described each of the wines. "Enjoy, gentlemen. I'll be right back with your tapas."

Ben and Rob each chose a glass and sipped, checking the notes for their particular wine. Then they switched glasses and sipped again. This continued until they each had tried all six wines.

"This is fun," Ben said. "Although I'm glad they're not large pours of wine."

"I agree. And these are tasty. Which ones do you like the best?"

Paulo returned with the tapas platter and a couple of small plates for them. He set them down and moved off to take care of some other people who had come in.

They sampled their drinks again, adding the food into the mix, to see how the wine's flavor changed with different items. They were careful to keep the glasses in the correct order so that they could accurately identify the wines.

By the time they finished both the wine and the food, they had decided on a couple of clear winners. Ben took a pen out of his pocket and handed it to Rob.

"Make notes on the cards so we can remember which ones we liked best."

After jotting down a few comments about the wines they enjoyed, Rob returned the pen to Ben, then folded the cards and stuck them in his pocket.

"Why don't we take a walk," Rob suggested.

They meandered along through Seaside Cove. As they

passed Waves seafood restaurant Rob asked, "Would you be interested in eating here this evening?"

"Sure, let's see if we can make a reservation now." Ben spoke with the host standing at the podium and was able to secure a table for them at nine-fifteen. With that done, they continued along with no particular route in mind.

Eventually, they found themselves on the Promenade Deck deciding to stop at the Mermaid's Tale Pub. There was a small seating area outside of the pub where they could have a drink and people-watch for a while.

I really love how things are developing between Rob and me. I feel whole when I'm with him. It's probably too soon to think about it, but I want to make plans to visit him as soon as I can. I wonder how he spends his holidays?

Ben caught Rob's eye and smiled. "Now that I've gotten the all-clear from Amanda, would it be okay if I held your hand?" he whispered.

A look of surprise swept across Rob's face, but he grinned and nodded shyly.

Ben took his hand and squeezed lightly. "Thank you."

After a few minutes, a quartet of musicians set up nearby and people began to gather in anticipation of the entertainment. They soon began playing, alternating between some light classical pieces and a few more modern compositions.

Ben and Rob sat together still holding hands, smiling, sipping their drinks, enjoying the music, and watching the world go by.

DINNER WAS, once again, wonderful. They shared oysters on the half shell and shrimp cocktail to start. Rob chose arctic char with roasted root vegetables for his main course, while Ben opted for Chilean sea bass with jasmine rice and snow peas. They split a bottle of Fumé Blanc and enjoyed a leisurely dinner together, occasionally sharing bites of each other's food.

After dinner, Rob and Ben slowly made their way back to Rob's cabin. Since they had left their bathing suits hanging in the shower earlier, the suits were now dry, so they undressed and put them on again.

Rob stepped out on to the balcony and realized how cool it was, but it was okay since they'd soon be warm in the hot tub. He flipped the jets on and grabbed a couple of towels before getting into the tub. Ben followed right behind, but instead of sitting next to Rob, he straddled him, kissing him soundly.

"Hi," he said, smiling.

"Hi yourself," Rob replied breathlessly, returning the kiss.

He opened up to Ben who began to suck on his tongue. "Mmm, you taste good," Ben said when he came up for air.

They continued to kiss, each giving and taking. Rob could feel their hard lengths beneath the water, separated by the thin material of their suits. Ben reached into Rob's suit and grasped his rigid cock. Lowering the suit, he tucked the waistband under Rob's balls and stroked him gently.

Rob tugged Ben's suit down until his ass was freed and then grabbed both cheeks and pulled them open, running a finger along his furry crack. They'd not turned the lights on, and the hot tub was on the side of the balcony facing the ocean, so they couldn't be seen at all from the Pool Deck.

Ben lifted Rob so that he was sitting on the edge of the tub then took Rob's length to the back of his throat. He pulled Rob's suit off the rest of the way and cupped his balls, allowing his fingers to wander back to Rob's hole.

Rob opened his legs wider and Ben teased his rim, at the same time sucking and licking Rob's cock. Rob leaned back, resting against the wall behind the hot tub. Raising Rob's legs a bit, Ben lowered his head, licking behind his balls until he reached Rob's hole.

Rob groaned and reached for his cock. He jerked himself while Ben licked and nipped, plunging his tongue into Rob.

"Coming!" Rob hissed, painting his stomach with his release. Ben stood and grabbed his own cock. Two strokes were all he needed until his own climax hit, his spunk joining Rob's. He leaned in, taking Rob's lips in a searing kiss.

He bent down and lapped at their mingled seed until Rob's belly was clean before kissing Rob again and lowering them back into the water to warm up.

"I'm really glad you wanted to use the hot tub again tonight, Ben. That was...fantastic!"

"Yeah, I manage to come up with a good idea now and again."

CHAPTER 13

Thursday, October 10 - Ajaccio, Corsica

Ben woke to find himself staring at Rob's sleeping visage. He smiled with happiness.

He's so handsome and absolutely adorable when he's sleeping. I could just look at him all day.

There was a bit of light peeking in through the drapes, so Ben knew it was morning, but he couldn't see the bedside clock and didn't want to turn over to reach his phone. He also didn't want to risk waking Rob up, so he kept still and continued to look at him with a goofy grin.

Eventually, he realized he really needed to pee, so he rose as gently as he could and went into the bathroom.

When he returned to bed, Rob's eyes were open. "Hi, sexy."

"Hi yourself," Ben replied. He glanced at the clock and saw that it was just after nine. "Are we going to be lazy today?"

"No, we're not," Rob said, laughing. "We're gonna shower and then have breakfast and then I was thinking maybe we could walk into town. Perhaps find a nice place to have lunch."

"Do you mean shower together?" Ben asked, his eyes twinkling.

"Of course. Saving water is a good thing, right?"

Ben turned on the water in the shower, letting it warm up before they stepped in. They washed each other's hair then Rob lathered Ben's body. He took a little extra time on Ben's cock and balls, then moved around to his ass and lingered in his crack, teasing his hole. They kissed, then Ben had his turn soaping up Rob everywhere.

Before they could go any further, Ben's stomach growled. Rob laughed, "I think someone needs to be fed."

They rinsed off and then dried each other, both still semi-hard. But they had things to do and places to go, so they behaved themselves.

Once they were dressed, they walked to the Bluefin Bistro to see if they could get a table for breakfast. Since they were in port, the restaurant wasn't crowded so they were seated immediately.

They ordered ham, cheddar, and mushroom omelets with hash brown potatoes and whole grain toast. While they waited, they sipped their coffee and Ben asked, "Have you been to Corsica before?"

"No, I haven't. That's why I thought about going into town today. Have you been here before?"

"No. It's gonna be fun exploring a new place together, isn't it?"

"Absolutely," Rob replied, face glowing with excitement. "I was reading the port information, the center of town is only about half a kilometer from the port, so that's an easy walk. We can do some exploring and have lunch, and I might try to find a little something for Sam."

"Oh, I meant to ask you where the next cruise was going. I kind of thought you might hit one of the ports that we went to before heading across the Atlantic."

Rob shook his head. "We're not going back to any of those ports, actually. That's why I thought I'd look for something here. We're stopping at three ports in Spain: Málaga, Cartagena, and Cádiz. I think there might be a day at sea in between each one, and we also stop in Tenerife. Then we cross, so that's seven more days at sea."

"And you fly home from Fort Lauderdale?" asked Ben.

"Yeah, but not until the next day. We're staying over at a hotel for one night and then we'll fly home the next afternoon."

After breakfast, they stopped by Ben's suite so that he could pick up his backpack. They saw his cabin attendant in the hall and reminded them that he was staying with Rob and not to worry about his suite. When he had last been there yesterday to pick up some clothes, he told them that he wouldn't be around much and gave them a nice tip, hoping they wouldn't think it was odd for him to stay somewhere else. But the more Ben thought about it, the more he realized that they'd probably seen stranger things on past cruises.

Back at Rob's suite, they freshened up and Rob got his backpack out of the closet. He then grabbed two bottles of water from the fridge and handed one to Ben. The day was sunny, but a bit breezy, so they both chose light jackets. If it got too warm later, they could carry the jackets in their backpacks.

"Ready?" Ben asked.

"Yeah, let's go."

TIME FLEW AS they walked around town with no real purpose other than seeing the sights and shopping.

Rob had found a beautiful silver and glass pendant on a black silk cord for Sam. And Ben saw a colorful scarf that he thought Amanda would like. He picked a similar one for Julie and bought them both. In their travels through the streets of the Ajaccio, they noticed Melissa and Don from their Tuscania tour, and they waved at each other as they wandered along.

After a while, they found a little park area and sat for a spell on a bench so they could watch people and enjoy the sights and sounds of life in the town.

After some time had passed, Rob asked, "Do you want to get some lunch?"

"Yeah, I could eat." Ben pointed across the main street toward the water. "It looks like there may be a few restaurants down that way."

"Okay, lead the way."

They checked out the menus posted outside each place they passed until finally picking one. The building was made of stone and the dining room had high ceilings and a fireplace in the corner. They were seated near windows that overlooked the water.

Rob seemed a bit quieter than usual, but Ben didn't make a big deal out of it. He thought Rob might be thinking about how the cruise would end in a couple of days and so let Rob have his space.

After a delicious lunch of fresh seafood and some local wine, they strolled back to the ship.

"So," Rob started, "The other day you said that you'd need to make a decision about whether or not to make some kind of public statement about us. Have you thought any more about that?"

Ah, so this is what's spinning around in that brain of his.

"I have actually, but I didn't want to make a decision on my own. I mean, it really does affect both of us, so I think it's a decision we should make together."

"Thanks, but isn't it more about you and your career?"

"I'm flattered that you think that, but you're important to me and I don't want to do anything that might negatively affect us. You and I agreeing on what's best for us is so much more important to me."

Rob grinned, "You're so caring, thinking about us and not only yourself. I'm fine with you making a public announcement, if you think that's the best way to go. Just get it all out there in the open, otherwise folks might get the idea that you're scared or ashamed or something. And I don't think that's healthy."

"Why am I not surprised that you were thinking that way? You try to hide it, but you're a very brave man, Rob. You want to face things head-on and just deal with them so that it's all open and aboveboard."

"Hmm," Rob interrupted. "I sense a 'but' coming."

"Not at all," Ben said. "I agree with you. I might not have a year ago, or hell, even a month ago. But in the short time I've known you, you made me realize that I don't want to hide this. I'm not afraid as long as you're in my corner."

"Whew!" Rob gasped with relief. "Good. I'm glad that we agree on this. If you had said no, I'd have gone along with you, but I really do feel this is the best way to handle it. This has been bugging me all day. I'm glad I asked you about it."

"I know it has," Ben said. "You've been unusually quiet; I knew something was going on in your head. I just wasn't sure what. But I was trying to give you a little time to work it out. I was probably gonna say something later if you didn't bring it up."

"You know me so well, already. That's just more confirmation to me that we're doing the right thing. Are you gonna talk to Amanda about this when you see her next week?"

"Definitely." Ben assured him. "It's the first order of business as far as I'm concerned. She'll probably suggest some kind of statement on social media pretty quickly. So I need to ask you, do you have a problem with me starting this while you're still on the cruise with Sam? I'll wait if you'd prefer, but part of me just wants to tell the world as soon as I can."

"I'm fine with that. Just text me and give me a heads-up or something so that I know it's gonna happen, okay?" Rob asked.

"Absolutely. I promise I won't blindside you. Can I use a photo of us? Maybe one of the selfies we took in Tuscania?" Ben looked hopeful that Rob would let him use a photo of them together.

"Yes, you can use a photo of your choosing. And I guess I should let my brother and sister know so that they don't learn about it in the news or something."

"Good idea. And I'll call my brother and Kyle. I guess I should tell Caroline, too."

BEN WAS SITTING in the living room of Rob's suite, checking his texts and emails. Rob had decided to take a nap when they got back, but Ben hadn't felt tired. He saw a text from his brother and decided that this might be a good time to tell him about Rob.

He dialed his brother's number and when Michael answered he said, "Hey Mikey, got a minute?"

"Of course," Michael groaned at the childhood nickname. "What's wrong? Not enjoying your cruise?"

"Actually, I'm having a better time than I ever expected. I ah...well actually, I met someone and wanted to let you know, since it's possible you may see something online or something."

"This sounds serious. Did you meet while you were promoting your movie or on the cruise?"

Ben paused and took a breath, "I met him in Barcelona, and it turns out we were both on this cruise."

Mike paused a few seconds before replying. "Him? Wow, that hasn't happened to you in quite a while. You really like this guy, huh?"

Ben loved how Mike just accepted the fact that it was a guy with no judgement. He felt his shoulders relax. "I haven't felt like this in a very long time. And it freaked me out a little since it happened so quickly. But it just feels so right. And he feels it too. His name is Rob, by the way. He's a widower from Massachusetts. His husband passed away a couple of years ago and he wasn't expecting anything like this either. "

"I'm happy for you, Ben. It sounds like this is a really good thing for both of you. But you said that I might see something online. Did someone take a photo of you two kissing or something?" Mike asked.

"No, but I talked to Amanda a couple of days ago to tell her what was going on. I don't think anyone's taken any photos and we haven't really been public about things, but you know how people are. I figured I'd let her know just in case. She said not to worry about it, and she'd run interference if something hit her radar.

"But we also discussed making a formal announcement of some sort. Rob and I talked about that earlier today and when I see Amanda next week, we'll figure out how to handle that. Probably a post on Twitter or Instagram or something with a photo of us."

"Cool. Again, I'm happy for you and hope this works out well for everyone. And bring him around to meet your older brother, okay?"

"I will, thanks. Love you, Mike."

"Love you too, Benny."

As the call ended, it was Ben's turn to groan at his nickname.

Might as well call Kyle, too.

"Hi, Dad. Everything going okay?"

"Everything's fine, son. I just wanted to share some news with you..." Their conversation was pretty much identical to the one he just had with Mike. But then, Ben hadn't expected anything less. Kyle wasn't fazed at all when Ben had told him a few years ago that he was attracted to both men and women.

He checked his watch and saw that he had another hour before Rob's alarm would go off. Snuggling sounded like a really good idea.

———

They were both rather contemplative when they woke. Ben told Rob about calling Michael and Kyle and while they were both happy with their non-reaction to Ben meeting a man, the fact that the cruise was ending in a few days hung ominously over their heads. And that left them feeling a little out of sorts.

Ben didn't want to dwell on what was to come all evening, so he changed the subject. "Let's see if we can get a table at the Bluefin Bistro for dinner and then maybe we can catch the show in the Ocean Theater afterwards. It's a musical variety show this evening. Or there's Doubloon Bay Casino, although I'm not much of a gambler."

"I don't gamble either, so the show sounds like a great idea to me."

After dinner they made their way to the theater. The show was quite good, proving to be exactly the distraction they both needed. Afterwards, they decided to stop at the Trident Lounge for a drink. Lukas saw them walk to the bar and he welcomed them and took their drink order. After getting their drinks, they moved to a table and sat, enjoying the bourbon on the rocks they'd both ordered.

"Despite all the people and activity going on here, I'm gonna miss this spot. There's something about it that's just so relaxing," Ben said.

"I agree. I don't know what it is, but this area just makes me feel calm."

When their glasses were empty, they slowly made their way back to Rob's suite.

They took turns in the bathroom, then climbed into bed. They were both tired and still feeling a bit melancholy, but they snuggled together and were soon asleep.

CHAPTER 14

Rob awoke with light streaming across his eyes from the partially opened drapes. He rolled over to find himself staring at the back of Ben's head. Reaching around, he pulled Ben into a hug, running his fingers through the hair on his chest.

"Good morning," Ben moaned sleepily.

"I'm sorry. Did I wake you?" Rob kissed Ben's shoulder and reveled in his familiar scent.

"I don't think you're sorry at all." He lifted Rob's hand from his chest and kissed it lightly. "So, what do you want to do today?"

"Just hang out with you, if that's okay. If Sam wasn't boarding the ship tomorrow, I think I'd just leave with you."

Ben twisted around until he was facing Rob. "Hey, it's

gonna be okay. I've got so much to do for the next week or so and you'll be home before you know it. And we can video chat and text while you and Sam are on the ship.

"Once you get home, we'll look at our schedules and figure out when we can get together again. And if things work out with one of the plays I've been approached about, I may end up in New York really soon."

"Yeah, you're right. I'm just not happy about saying goodbye tomorrow. I've gotten used to having you around and I like it. A lot." Rob said with a heavy sigh.

"It's not goodbye, it's just so long for a little while. We'll make this work. I promise."

"I believe you. Now, what about breakfast?"

***

THE DAY PASSED QUIETLY. They walked around a bit as Ben tried to commit to memory all the places on the ship they had spent time together. He took a few photos of just Rob as well as a couple of selfies of them together. He got an especially nice one of Rob near the waterfall in Seaside Cove and set that as his phone's wallpaper.

"Okay, now I need one of you."

Rob pulled out his phone and took several photos of Ben. Ben stuck his tongue out for a goofy one, making Rob giggle, then he managed to take one where Ben wasn't looking directly at the camera. He was smiling and looked thoughtful, like he was daydreaming. Rob chose that one for his wallpaper. Showing his phone to Ben, he said, "I think you look especially handsome in this one."

THEY'D ENJOYED a nice dinner of grilled steak, shrimp and fried rice in the Teppanyaki dining room at Kaiyo but skipped dessert and after-dinner drinks. No sooner had they entered Rob's suite, and Ben was all over him. They kissed passionately, their tongues battling for control. Ben unbuttoned Rob's shirt, circling his nipples with his thumbs.

Rob moaned, reaching for Ben's belt buckle. Undoing it and pulling down the zipper on his trousers, he reached in and stroked Ben's cock through his underwear. He could feel the wet spot where Ben was already leaking. They moved into the bedroom and continued stripping until they were both naked and fully aroused.

"You are so beautiful," Ben said, lowering Rob onto the bed and climbing on top of him.

"Please Ben, I want you tonight," Rob whispered.

"Are you sure? I don't want to rush things."

"I want this," Rob whispered. "So much."

Ben walked into the bathroom and returned with a condom and small bottle of lube that he'd found earlier in his toiletry kit. He set them on the nightstand then looked at Rob and gently said, "Let me get you ready."

Kissing him deeply, Ben moved his way down Rob's body with slow kisses, licking and nipping at his nipples, first one, then the other. He dipped his tongue into Rob's navel, then buried his nose in the space between Rob's thigh and balls, inhaling his scent.

Kissing the head of his cock tenderly, he opened his mouth and sucked him down, at the same time twisting each nipple with his thumb and forefinger. Ben moaned around the hard cock in his mouth and Rob whimpered.

"Please, Ben," he begged.

Ben moved off Rob's cock and moved lower, sucking each ball into his mouth. Then lower still. He raised Rob's legs, kissing behind his balls and licking at his hole. He plunged his tongue deep, teasing and nibbling the rim, as Rob squirmed.

"Ungh, mmmm, ahhh..." Rob moaned incoherently.

Ben reached for the lube and squirted a bit on his fingers, then probed Rob's hole slowly and steadily.

"More, please," Rob begged, and Ben obliged with a second finger.

He sucked the head of Rob's cock, swiping his tongue around the crown. Then he released Rob's cock and moved up to claim his mouth in a smoldering kiss. He added a third finger and continued to dip in and out, scissoring them to open Rob up even more.

Rob reached for the condom and tore open the package. He took his time rolling it down Ben's aching cock before adding some lube to slick Ben's dick and pleaded, "Please, Ben, now!"

Ben withdrew his fingers from Rob's body and guided his rigid length into his waiting hole. He breached Rob slowly, inching forward as they gazed into each other's eyes.

"Yes. So good," Rob whispered. "More."

Once his balls rested against Rob's ass, Ben stopped, waiting for Rob to adjust to the feel of him deep inside.

"Okay?" he asked, making sure he wasn't hurting Rob at all.

"Perfect. You feel so fucking good inside of me."

Ben began to move slowly, pulling almost all the way out

until only the tip of his cock remained in Rob. Then he slid back in, gently fucking him. He slowly built up speed, adjusting his position slightly so that he filled Rob deeper, hitting his prostate.

"Yes!" screamed Rob, "That's it. Again!"

Ben thrust into Rob, driving even faster. "Not gonna last," he panted. Then, a moment later, "Oh fuck, I'm coming!"

He filled the condom as he climaxed. He kissed Rob breathlessly. Wetness touched his belly and Ben looked down. The hair around his navel was covered in Rob's cum. Rob kissed him and exhaled heavily.

"Oh my God, I don't think I've ever come so hard. And definitely not without touching my dick."

"That was amazing. It's never felt that perfect for me before." Ben admitted, his breath slowing.

Ben pulled out carefully, gripping the condom. He removed it, tying off the end, then walked into the bathroom and threw it in the wastebasket. He returned with a warm, wet washcloth and a small towel. He cleaned and dried Rob, then himself, dropping the cloth and towel on the floor beside the bed.

"Do you think we might be able to switch it up next time?" Rob asked. "As amazing as that was, and I'd definitely like to do it again, variety is the spice of life, isn't it?"

"Oh, we most certainly can switch it up. I can't wait."

Turning off the light, he reached for Rob and claimed one more kiss.

CHAPTER 15

Rob had been lying awake for some time, looking at Ben as he slept. It was their last day together for a while, but Rob was determined to not make it weird or sad. The night before had been fantastic. He replayed it in his head, remembering the love and passion he felt for the man lying next to him. He searched his feelings, wondering if he'd feel any guilt, but finding none. There was simply a feeling of complete contentment.

They still had today together, and Rob was excited for Ben and Sam to meet, so it was going to be a good day. Plus, he and Ben would see each other again soon. It wasn't a sad day at all.

Maybe if I keep telling myself that, I'll start to believe it.

"You're looking at me, aren't you?" Ben said, his eyes still closed.

"Maybe," Rob replied, smiling. "I wish we could stay here forever, but we really do need to get up."

They showered in unison, enjoying their time together. But aside from some hot kisses, they managed to keep it PG. The night before would live in their memories and keep them going until they could meet up again.

Ben packed his things into his small rolling carry-on and his backpack, and they set off for the Bluefin Bistro, which was designated as a debarkation lounge for suite passengers. They snagged some coffee and a muffin, then found a seat to wait for their announcement to depart the ship.

Normally, Rob would have had to wait to leave until passengers ending their cruise had all disembarked. But he had spoken with the suite concierge the day before. He'd explained that he needed to meet Sam at her hotel and had been able to obtain permission to depart a bit earlier than normal. A member of the crew would come get him and escort him out with some passengers heading out on an excursion. Ben would depart when his section was called, and they would meet outside.

After approximately twenty minutes, Ben's section was called, "Okay, that's me. I'll see you outside in a little while."

Not long after Ben had departed, a crew member entered the lounge and called Rob's name. They left together and met the other passengers in the Coral Reef Lounge. Once they'd left the ship, Rob thanked the crew member and separated from the group.

He walked around looking for the area where cars were waiting to pick up departing passengers. He spotted a driver with a sign reading Rockingham, so he walked closer and stood to the side.

Pulling out his phone, he texted Ben.

> I've located your car and driver. Waiting off to the side. C U soon.

Not expecting a reply, he put his phone back into his pocket, but a moment later, it buzzed.

> When I called them yesterday to extend my reservation for most of the day, I gave them your name, so you can go and sit in the car if you'd like. I'm almost at the front of the customs line and should be out soon.

Rob smiled at Ben's thoughtfulness and walked to the car. The driver spotted him and asked, "Señor Rockingham?"

"No, I'm Rob Asher, I'm meeting Mr. Rockingham here. I just texted him and he should be here in a few minutes."

"Very good, señor Asher. I am Gustavo, but you may call me Gus. Would you like to sit in the car to wait for señor Rockingham?"

"Thank you, but the fresh air feels good, so I'll wait out here."

They chatted a bit and Rob told Gus that he was getting back on the ship later that day with Sam to sail to the United States. After a few minutes, Rob's phone buzzed again.

> Heading out. Where R U?

Rob typed a quick message explaining where to look and he scanned the doors to the pier facility. As soon as he saw Ben, he waved, and Ben started toward the car.

Rob pointed to him and said to Gus, "That's him."

Gus hurried to help Ben with his luggage. Bags secured in the trunk and Ben and Rob in the back seat, the car headed to the hotel.

***

As Ben checked in, Rob texted Sam.

At the hotel. Where R U?

In my room. Just finished packing my suitcase. Should I meet U downstairs or do U want to come up? #407

I'll be up shortly. Bringing a friend.

Yes!

As Ben walked over to him, Rob mentioned, "Sam's in her room. Let's drop off your luggage. Then we'll head to her room so you two can meet."

A few minutes later, Rob knocked on Sam's door. The door practically flew open and Sam stood there, looking radiant, as always.

Samantha Martinez was five-seven and gorgeous. She had long, dark hair and deep-brown eyes. Her olive skin glowed with minimal makeup, and her smile reached her eyes. She wore navy slacks and a silk blouse in a floral pattern of navy and cream with a pop of bright orange.

She hugged Rob tightly and kissed his cheek. "Oh my God, he's so hot," she whispered to Rob. Then she extended a manicured hand to Ben and said, "Hi, I'm Sam and I know you're Ben. It's such a pleasure to meet you."

They shook hands and Sam pulled him in for a hug. In a stage whisper Sam said, "If you break his heart, I'll hurt you. There are some woods on his property, and I know just where to bury the body. They'll never find you." She smiled widely at Ben.

Rob laughed and they all joined in. "Stop it Sam. I just managed to convince him that he wants me. Don't scare him away!"

Ben looked at Rob and said, "Oh my God, she *is* loyal. I like her!" Then he turned to Sam, "I have no intentions of hurting him, Sam. I just want to make him happy if he'll let me." He spoke softly and sincerely.

"That means a lot to me, Ben" Sam admitted quietly. "I assume that we'll soon be the best of friends. It's not easy keeping this guy out of his own head sometimes." She gestured at Rob.

"Tell me about it. And yes, I expect that we'll get along famously. Rob probably hasn't told you," Ben continued, "but you're spending the afternoon with two handsome men."

"Yeah, but they clearly only have eyes for each other. Story of my life," Sam joked.

Ben was undeterred. "We're going to have a brief driving tour of the city just to kill a little bit of time and then we'll have a leisurely lunch. After that, the driver will drop me back here and take the two of you to the pier. Why don't we leave your luggage in my room and we can pick it up later?"

Gus drove them around the city for a little more than an hour. Sam had arrived in Barcelona two days earlier but hadn't done much in the way of sightseeing yet, so it was a great way to see a lot in a short amount of time. Surprisingly, she'd not been to Barcelona before, but after this quick tour, she told them that she was determined to come back as soon as she could.

When Gus dropped them off at the restaurant for lunch, he said to Ben, "I'll be back in a couple of hours. If you need me before that, call me and I'll return immediately." He handed Ben a card with his contact information.

The threesome entered the restaurant and Ben walked up to the podium. *"Tengo una reserva para tres a nombre de Rockingham."*

"Ah, señor Rockingham. Welcome back. Please follow me."

The restaurant was quiet, and they were seated at a table near large windows facing the Mediterranean Sea.

"Ben and I ate here the night before the cruise and the food is wonderful. Do you want to share some appetizers to start?" Rob asked Sam.

"Yes, but please choose whatever you want. You know what I like, Rob."

"How about some *jamón* and the grilled shrimp? Maybe some oysters, too?"

When the waiter arrived at their table, Ben took care of ordering the appetizers along with a bottle of Sauvignon Blanc. The menu featured a lunch special of roasted branzino served on a bed of sauteed vegetables and they all decided on that for their entrée. They took their time eating and chatting and at one point, Ben ordered a second bottle of wine.

"It seems like things are going well between the two of you," Sam remarked. "I'm so glad you got your head outta your ass and listened to me, Rob."

Rob chuckled. "You said it yourself Sam. I get stuck in my head sometimes. At least I had enough sense to call you when it happened this time."

"Thank you for talking him off the ledge that day, Sam," Ben added. "I was a mess for a good part of it too, although it was much worse for Rob. I'll never be able to repay you."

"Just keep him happy. That'll be payment enough as far as I'm concerned. He was in a bad place for too long. I'm so glad he found you."

"Excuse me," Rob said, rising. "I need to find the restroom."

As he walked away, Ben handed Sam a card and said, "Here's my email and cell number. Rob's been fine these past few days and I don't expect anything to happen. But I'd like you to have a way to get in touch if you need to."

"Thanks," Sam said. She put the card in her purse and handed her own to Ben. "And here's my info in case you need to reach me."

She looked at him thoughtfully. "You really care for him, don't you?"

"I..." Ben started.

Sam cut him off. "Don't bother trying to deny it, I can see it in your eyes. More importantly, I know that Rob cares deeply for you. I see it every time he looks at you. I haven't seen him look at anyone like that since Alan died. So, thank you for bringing that light back into his eyes. But," she paused, then continued, "what happens next? You do live on opposite coasts, after all."

"Well, the first thing that happens is that I meet with my agent next week and we discuss a plan for me to make some kind of announcement on social media about the new man in my life."

Sam looked at him, surprised.

"And before you say anything, yes, Rob and I talked about this and we both want it. I wouldn't do anything to make Rob uncomfortable. The other option is to just let it come out naturally, but that could cause more commotion in the media and neither one of us wants to give the impression that we're hiding this."

"I suppose that makes sense."

Rob returned to the table. "What are you guys talking about?"

"Ben was just telling me how he'll make an announcement about you on social media. Rob, are you sure you're okay with this?"

"Yes, Sam. This is exactly the right way to do this. We're not hiding so the quicker folks hear about it the better. Really, it's gonna be okay."

"Okay, I trust both of you." She turned to Ben laughing. "But remember, I will hurt you if I need to!"

CHAPTER 16

Saturday, October 12 - Barcelona, Spain, later the same day

Back at the hotel, Ben told Gus that Rob and Sam would return shortly for their ride to the cruise port.

When they got to Ben's room, Sam used the bathroom to freshen up, then hugged and kissed Ben. "It was wonderful meeting you, Ben. I look forward to seeing you again soon. Have a safe flight home.

"Okay," she continued, speaking to both of them. "I'm going downstairs to wait for you in the lobby. I don't need to be here for your goodbyes. Just don't start something you can't finish." She smirked, grabbed her rolling suitcase, and walked out the door.

Ben moved closer to Rob, enveloping him in a hug. They remained like that for a minute, gently swaying. Rob kissed him tenderly, hugging him tighter. He didn't want to let go. The kisses became more heated—teasing, tasting, trying to memorize each other. Ben could feel Rob's hard-on against his own. Rob's shoulders shook with quiet sobs.

Ben was tempted to drop to his knees, but he held back. He knew he needed to calm down and keep Rob from falling apart.

"Hey, look at me, Rob," he said, staring into Rob's tear-filled eyes. "This isn't goodbye. I promise I'll see you very soon. And in the meantime, we'll talk. You can call me or text me anytime you want. Time zones be damned."

"Okay." Rob agreed with a sniffle. "And you can call or text me, too. I know this isn't goodbye. I just wasn't ready for it to feel like this. I know it's too early to use the L-word, but you're already in my heart, Ben."

Rob leaned in for another passionate kiss; Ben could almost feel the love radiating from him.

"And you're in mine, sweetheart." Ben echoed in between more kisses. "Now go and wash your face so that Sam doesn't come back upstairs and beat my ass when she sees you."

Rob grinned, went into the bathroom, and did as he was told.

Walking back into the room, he embraced Ben one last time, kissing him soundly.

EPILOGUE

Saturday, October 26 - Fort Lauderdale, Florida

am and Rob were sitting in the Bluefin Bistro. It had once again been designated as a debarkation lounge for suite passengers, so they were patiently waiting to be told they could leave.

The last two weeks had been both wonderful and trying. The first few days were especially difficult. Rob missed Ben so much, but Sam was a trooper and kept him from getting lost in his head.

Sam and Rob had enjoyed an amazing cruise. They had fun exploring a few ports in Spain and then spent a lot of time reading and sunbathing on the balcony of their suite. They ate well at all of the ship's restaurants and drank often—so many drinks. But they had fun, and with Sam steadying Rob, his heart didn't hurt at all.

Ben and Rob texted several times each day and had even broken down and chatted via FaceTime twice. They were still trying to come up with a plan to get together but hadn't finalized anything yet. Ben had been extremely busy as soon as he got back to LA.

With Amanda's help, they had crafted an announcement that Ben posted on Twitter and Instagram with a photo of himself and Rob. It caused a flurry of questions but was generally well-received with only a few negative comments in the media. Between that and the interviews about the upcoming movie, life for Ben had been hectic.

Ben had told Rob when it would happen, so Rob had texted and then spoke with his brother and sister. Both Geoff and Megan were a bit surprised, but happy for Rob and completely supportive. *Life was good.*

It looked like Ben would be heading to New York in a few weeks to meet with some folks about appearing in a new play, so he and Rob had made tentative plans to get together then either in New York, Massachusetts, or both.

One morning, Rob and Sam were sitting on a bench in Seaside Cove when Melissa, from the Tuscania excursion, walked up to him and showed him the photo Ben had posted on Instagram.

"I thought there was something going on between the two of you," she said, smiling. "But you were both so coy about it all. Anyway, I'm really happy for you both and screw anyone who doesn't like it. Everyone deserves to be happy."

Rob was a bit gob-smacked by that but managed to utter a sincere "thank you" before Melissa strolled away.

ROB WAS SCANNING the pick-up area outside of the cruise terminal for a driver waiting to take him and Sam to their hotel. He had received a confirmation email that morning, so it was just a matter of locating the driver.

"Rob, is that the driver?" Sam asked, pointing to a woman standing near a black SUV and holding a sign. "I think her sign says Asher. Rob glanced over and sure enough, that was his name on the sign. They quickly got the luggage into the back and were soon on their way to their hotel.

Rob really hated flying home the same day he got off a ship. He preferred to get a hotel for a day or two and make the vacation last just a little longer. So, he and Sam were spending the day in Fort Lauderdale. Sam would probably want to hang out by the pool this afternoon, and that was fine with him. They planned on having dinner at Giovanni's that night—it was his favorite here—and they'd fly north the next afternoon.

They checked in and headed to their rooms. While they had sometimes shared a room in the past, Sam had insisted on her own room today. *"I've just spent two weeks sharing a suite with you on a ship, Rob. I think I'd like my own space."*

Rob suspected that she was giving him some space since he was planning to FaceTime with Ben. Far be it from her to cockblock him if he had an opportunity for some sexy times.

He opened his suitcase and pulled out slacks and a shirt to hang up so that he'd have something to wear for dinner. He grabbed his swimsuit and tossed it on a nearby chair, figuring he'd put it on after lunch and sunbathe with Sam for a while.

He had just put his toiletry kit on the bathroom counter when he heard a knock on his door.

Sam probably wants to go and find lunch somewhere.

He opened the door. "Lunchtime alrea—"

There stood Ben, holding a single red rose and smiling brightly, "To new adventures." He handed the rose to Rob, then stepped forward, enveloping Rob in a bear hug, kissing him deeply.

"What are you, um, how did…?" Rather than finish his thought, Rob kissed Ben back, and pulled him in tighter.

"I just couldn't wait to see you again. And fuck anyone who says it's too soon…I love you, Rob."

"I love you too, Ben. So much." Another minute or two passed. No talking, just lots of kissing. Finally Rob said, "I'm guessing Sam had something to do with this?"

"Yep, she and I have been texting for at least a week. I got in yesterday and I've been waiting for her message, so I knew what room you were in."

"Looks like I owe her flowers too."

"Already taken care of, sweetheart. She'll get two dozen roses delivered to her at work on Monday."

"Oh, you're good," Rob remarked, impressed.

"And I haven't told you the best part yet. I hope you're not mad, but I'm flying home with you tomorrow and we can hang out for a few days before I head to New York to meet with the director and producer I was telling you about."

"Best. News. Ever."

Just then Rob's phone buzzed. He pulled it out of his pocket and saw a text from Sam.

> You're welcome. I'm gonna grab some lunch and then I'll be at the pool. I'm sure you'll be occupied for the afternoon but hoping we can still do dinner. I called Giovanni's and changed the reservation already. Love U.

Rob laughed, showing the message to Ben. "Suddenly, I feel like I need a nap...or something," Rob said, kissing Ben passionately.

"Or something indeed."

The End

A Letter from RJ

Dear Reader,

Thank you so much for reading Love on the Horizon. The next book in this series is Love for the Holidays. Find out what happens when Rob and Ben decide to spent Christmas in England with family and friends. But what's a family holiday without a little drama?

Be sure to follow me on Amazon to be notified of new releases, and look for me on Facebook for sneak peeks of upcoming stories.

Please take a moment to write a review of Love on the Horizon on Amazon and Goodreads. Reviews can make all the difference in helping a book show up in Amazon searches.

To to sign up for my newsletter, stop by rj-peterson.ck.page.

We have a great reader group on Facebook that can be found here: www.facebook.com/groups/rjpetersonsadventurers/

Finally, several of my titles are available on audio, narrated by the amazing Kevin Earlywine or the fabulous Cole Kurtz. They can be found here: link.rjpeterson.net/audio

Happy reading!

RJ

P.S. Keep going for a free download!

FREE SHORT STORY

Download a copy of His Elevator Pitch

Inspired by a writing prompt, His Elevator Pitch is the story of River, an unemployed executive assistant, and Thom, the department head of a prestigious multi-faceted corporation.

When a power failure takes out several city blocks in Boston, MA, they find themselves stuck in an elevator with nothing but time on their hands.

Conversation ensues and when power is restored, River goes off to his interview, thinking that's the end of his encounter with the handsome stranger. Or is it?

This story features many of the themes my writing is known for: older guys, sweet-with-heat encounters, low or no angst, and always a happily ever after.

SCAN THE CODE TO DOWNLOAD

ABOUT THE AUTHOR

Hi, I'm RJ! I'm a retired graphic designer. An avid reader—preferably while sipping a vodka martini or bourbon on the rocks—I've had a long and varied career, including library page, car wash attendant, travel agent, and graphic designer in the marijuana industry. In addition, I worked in the banking industry for twenty-five years. I love to travel and have been on 60+ cruises. When not on a cruise, my husband & I live in New England.

I never planned to be a writer, but a fateful day in January, 2021 changed it all. I woke with a story stuck in my head and started typing. The more I type, the more story ideas I get.

Find all my links here:

WANT TO READ MORE?

The New Adventures in Love Series:

Love On The Horizon

Love For The Holidays

Love On The Potomac

Love In The Mediterranean

Love Is For Family

(Coming in 2025)

Hawthorne Bluff Series:

Finding Finlay

Addicted to Ashton

Chasing Courtland

(Coming in 2026)

SEAsons of Love Series:

Love at Frost Sight

Resting Grinch Face

Don't Claus a Scene

Great Chemis-Tree

Stand Alone Stories

The Locket's Tale

Footprints on My Heart

(Coming in 2025)

All my book links in one place!

www.ingramcontent.com/pod-product-compliance
Lightning Source LLC
Chambersburg PA
CBHW020759310726
48969CB00002B/612